MYSTERY AT HAW...
and other stories

GW00937867

Adventure, mystery, danger and suspense
are some of the ingredients in this
exciting new collection of action-packed
stories.

There's a Wild West adventure, a
futuristic space story and a spine-chilling
legend — and lots more!

Chris Spencer has written many stories
for children, including the space
adventure, *Starforce Red Alert*, also
published by Lion.

To Mum and Dad

Mystery at Hawktowers
and other stories

CHRIS SPENCER

A LION PAPERBACK
Tring · Belleville · Sydney

Published by
Lion Publishing plc
Icknield Way, Tring, Herts, England
ISBN 0 85648 819 4
Albatross Books Pty Ltd
PO Box 320, Sutherland, NSW 2232, Australia
ISBN 0 86760 670 3

First edition 1985

British Library Cataloguing in Publication Data
Spencer, Chris
    Mystery at Hawktowers and other stories.
    I. Title
    823'.914[J]   PZ7
    ISBN 0 85648 819 4

Printed and bound in Great Britain
by Cox & Wyman Ltd, Reading

CONTENTS

Mystery at
Hawktowers

'Would you believe it?' said Steve, looking out of the window as the train rocked and rattled through the Highlands. 'Our first trip to Scotland and it's raining.'

'Rats!' groaned Daniel. 'I hope we don't have to walk to Hawktowers in a downpour. That *would* make a good start to our summer holiday.'

There was a third boy in the carriage – a young Scot on his way home – and he smiled at the two dark-haired brothers with their bulging rucksacks beside them. He hadn't known them long – only since they had boarded the train together some hours earlier – but already he'd got used to their scheming ways. 'All right,' he said, 'I'm sure my father will give you a lift in the car. We have to go past the estate, anyway.'

Steve gave a big grin. 'That would be great, Alex.'

'On one condition,' the young Scot went on, for he was a bit of a schemer himself. 'You let me come and explore the grounds with you whenever I want, and that you show me the ospreys' nest so that I can take some photos. I've got a telephoto lens.'

Steve reached out his hand and Alex shook it. 'It's a deal. Agreed, Daniel?'

'Agreed,' Daniel replied. 'Assuming it's all right with the Laird, of course.'

'Och, Mr Baxter won't mind – he's a nice old boy. A bit eccentric sometimes, but he's friendly enough. Not that anyone sees much of him; he rarely leaves the estate.'

'A bit of a hermit, eh?' chuckled Steve, swaying with

the movement of the train.

Alex nodded. 'Aye. Anyway, it's McAllister who'll be sorting you out — telling you where to pitch your tent and all that.'

'Who's McAllister?' the brothers asked. The letter they had received from the Laird of Hawktowers, confirming that they could camp on the estate, hadn't mentioned any McAllister.

'He's the gamekeeper. They say he watches over the grounds like one of its own hawks. Probably have his eye on you two as well!'

'Us *three* you mean,' said Daniel. 'Anyway, what's he like, this McAllister?'

The boy laughed, a wicked twinkle in his blue eyes. 'He's a monster! Seven feet tall and two heads. Eats English kids for breakfast!' he said in his broadest Scottish accent.

Daniel whipped off the baseball cap he was wearing and flung it at him. 'You great haggis! Tell us what he's really like.'

'Hey, look,' said Steve, his face to the window as he tried to peer up the track. 'I think we're coming into our station.' Then he glanced up at the storm-filled sky. 'Don't fancy pitching a tent in this.'

Very soon they were stepping from the train and running for the shelter of the ticket office. 'You wait here,' Alex told them. 'I'll see if my father's arrived.' And even as he said it an old car came shuddering to a halt outside the doors. The driver wound down his window and smiled as Alex went towards him. Steve and Daniel noticed with surprise that the man at the wheel wore a clerical collar. 'He didn't say his dad was a vicar,' muttered Steve.

Daniel grinned. 'Reckon he'll take up a collection while we're driving along?'

Alex turned, smiling, and beckoned the brothers. His

father got out of the car. He was a plumpish man with a round, jolly face. 'Welcome to Scotland,' he said as he greeted them, and reached out for their rucksacks. 'We'll put these in the boot. Hop in now before you get soaked.'

'Thanks,' said Steve as they settled into the back seat. 'We really appreciate this.'

The vicar slammed his door shut. 'Well, you'd get drowned walking all the way to Hawktowers in this weather.' There was a small explosion as the engine fired, a cloud of smoke, and then they lurched forward. Steve and Daniel exchanged glances and smothered their amusement. What a welcome to Scotland!

As they drove, heading up into the hills, Alex briefly told his father about the great week he'd spent with his uncle down south, but he seemed just as excited about spending time with his new friends on their bird-watching and wildlife holiday.

'Aye, you'll have a grand time at Hawktowers,' his father told the boys over his shoulder, 'but just make sure you report to Mr McAllister at his lodge before you go pitching any tents or poking around. He's in charge of the estate and likes to keep things orderly.'

'So we've heard,' said Steve. 'Alex says he's a bit of a monster.'

The vicar glanced at his son beside him. 'Well, that's putting it a bit strong, Alex. He can be stern sometimes, I agree, but on the whole he's a reasonable sort. Just keep on the right side of him and you've nothing to fear.'

They drove on through the rain, climbing up through dense woodland, and presently the vicar switched on the car radio. The news programme had just started and, without paying any attention, the boys heard about the latest developments in a dockers' strike, a plane crash somewhere in Spain, the visit of African heads of state to Britain, and something about a girl who'd been kidnapped near her school while on a cross-country run a few days ago. She was the daughter of a wealthy industrialist and apparently the kidnappers were demanding two million pounds for her release. After the weather report the vicar turned the radio off. He was shaking his head about something. 'Terrible thing, these kidnappings. That young lassie is going to need our prayers if she's to be returned without harm. So often these things end in tragedy.'

'Och, she'll be all right if her dad coughs up the money,' said Alex.

His father said no more and they drove on in silence for a while. Before long they left the trees behind and the road took them high into the hills. The boys couldn't see much through the rain-spattered windows but their driver told them they were passing through some of the loveliest countryside in the kingdom. 'These hills, the lochs below, the miles of forestland, and away down there to our left is the coast. Aye, the Good Lord didn't stint when he made this part of the world.'

Steve and Daniel mumbled their general agreement; they weren't really interested in the view – that is, until the old car topped a hill and Alex told them they would soon be able to see Hawktowers in the valley below. When they reached the spot the vicar slowed down and the boys wound down their windows.

'Cor!' said Steve. 'It's huge!'

Hawktowers was spread out below them like a great relief map with the old stone manor house nestling in a vast bowl of greenery and woodland. There were over two thousand acres in all, the vicar told them.

'Fancy having all that to yourself!' muttered Daniel. 'There must be *hundreds* of species in those woods. Look out for the ospreys, Steve.'

'Right. Is that a trout stream running through the grounds? That's where they'll be.' But then something else caught the boy's eye. 'See that little house down towards the road, on the far side?'

'Must be the gamekeeper's lodge,' Daniel replied.

'Aye,' said the vicar. 'That's where you should report. We'll be there in just a few minutes now.'

'Is that the sea beyond that next ridge of hills?' asked Steve. It was difficult to tell through the heavy rain and low cloud.

'That's right,' said Alex, 'and if you look over there, where there's a dip between two hills, you can just see the fishing village where you'll be getting your supplies. It's a quaint old place with hilly streets and an old harbour. I'll show you round it sometime, if you like.'

They were still taking in the scene as the car gathered speed again, this time dropping down along the road that skirted round the estate. After a while they passed a little stone church high up off the road – one of the churches Alex's father was responsible for – and from there the road fell steeply away into the valley. At the foot of the hill the road swung round in a curve and levelled out, running alongside the high stone wall that marked the Hawktowers boundary, and eventually leading to the estate's main entrance where high wrought-iron gates stood permanently open.

'I'll leave you here,' said Alex's father. 'It's only a short walk down the drive to the lodge, and it looks as if the rain's letting up now.'

'Thanks,' said Steve. 'And don't forget, Alex – come along any time you want. I expect McAllister will tell you where to find us.'

'If he hasn't eaten you!' the boy laughed.

His father got out and handed the lads their rucksacks from the boot. 'Have a good holiday,' he said. And then the car was gone, disappearing down the road in a cloud of smoke with Alex waving out of the window.

'Here at last!' said Daniel as they both pulled on their waterproofs.

11

Two minutes later they were inside the grounds, knocking at the gamekeeper's lodge. But there was no reply.

'Try again,' said Steve. 'It's gone five o'clock. You'd think he'd be at home with his feet up by now.'

No one came to the door, however, and after a few minutes they decided to set off up the drive, intending to call at the manor house. But they had not gone ten yards when a shout stopped them in their tracks.

'Hold it right there!'

The gruff voice made them jump, but they had an even bigger shock when they swung round to find themselves looking down the barrels of a shotgun. Its owner, a broad, granite-faced man wearing an oilskin coat and soiled peaked cap, had emerged from the trees behind the lodge and stood pinning them to the spot with his fierce eyes as much as with his gun.

'Trespassers get one chance,' he snarled. 'Now be off with you − and fast.'

'We − we're not trespassing,' said Daniel, his voice suddenly squeaky. 'We've got a letter from − '

'I don't care what you've got,' the man growled. 'This is private property and you're leaving.'

'But the Laird's expecting us,' Steve explained. 'We've got a letter to prove it − he said we could stay here in the grounds.'

The man cocked a bushy eyebrow. 'Oh aye? Expecting you, is he?'

Daniel fumbled in his rucksack. 'It's right here, the letter.' He found it and held it out, not daring to move from the spot because the gun was still pointing at him.

'Let's be seeing it, then.'

Daniel edged forward and was relieved when the gamekeeper finally lowered his gun and reached out for the letter.

The boys exchanged anxious glances while the fierce

eyes scanned the piece of paper. When he stopped reading he folded the letter and slid it into his pocket.

'Birdwatchers, are you? Well, there's been a change of plan. The Laird's had trouble with kids like you just lately and he doesn't want any more bother. Now clear off.'

'But we're not going to make any trouble,' Daniel persisted. 'We only want to study the ospreys and – '

'Oh, it's the ospreys you'll be wanting, is it? No doubt to steal their eggs, eh?'

'Eggs? But – '

'No buts.' He cocked the shotgun. 'You're not wanted, is that clear? Now get lost before I throw you out.'

'What about our letter?' demanded Steve.'

'Move!'

'All right,' said Daniel, grabbing his brother's sleeve. 'We're going. Come on, Steve.'

'But – '

'Come *on*!'

They were barely out of the man's earshot before Steve grabbed Daniel by the shoulder. 'What did you do that for? We should have insisted on seeing the Laird. Now where are we going to camp tonight?'

Daniel didn't answer until they were beyond the main gates. 'Are you daft? He would never let us see the Laird.'

'Why not?'

'For one thing because he's a nutter, pointing that gun at us. And for another I'm not trusting a gamekeeper who doesn't know his job.'

'What? What are you talking about?'

The boy glanced quickly back up the drive. 'Look, that bloke's supposed to be a gamekeeper and he doesn't even know about ospreys.'

Steve only stared at him.

'The eggs,' said Daniel, lowering his voice. 'You heard

13

him – he thought we were after osprey eggs, but they would have hatched weeks ago.'

'All right,' said Steve impatiently, 'I'll admit it sounds a bit odd, but right now I'm more interested in where we're going to camp tonight. We haven't even got the Laird's letter now to prove we should be staying there.'

'Yeah, that was mean of him,' grumbled Daniel. 'But it's not going to do us any good now, anyway. The best thing we can do is find a call-box and phone the Laird. He's bound to sort it out for us – or at least he'll tell us where we can stay if he really doesn't want anyone camping on the estate.'

Steve agreed to the plan. 'I think there was a call-box up the hill by the church, wasn't there? It's a bloomin' long walk, though.'

'Then let's get started. At least the rain's almost stopped.'

'We should have asked Alex's dad to wait,' said Steve. '*He'd* have sorted McAllister out, I bet.'

'Well, it's too late now. Come on.'

They found the call-box twenty minutes later, but it did them no good. The Laird of Hawktowers was not on the phone.

'Talk about eccentric,' scoffed Steve. 'You'd think the old boy could at least have a phone, stuck out here miles from anywhere. Anyway, what are we going to do now?'

Daniel stood looking around, up and down the road. 'I think there's a farm just a bit higher up. Remember passing it on the way down? We'll try there.'

'All right. I only hope the farmers round here are a bit more friendly than the gamekeepers. Alex was right – that McAllister is a monster.'

To their relief the farmer was friendly. He pointed to a field behind the farmhouse. 'You can pitch your tent anywhere in there,' he told them, 'and I've eggs and milk if you need them. Be sure to ask.'

14

They chose a sheltered place high in the field, where there was a view over the valley, over the Hawktowers estate. By climbing a tree they could see over the pine forest to the tips of the four stone towers that marked each corner of the old manor house – the towers that had given the estate its name, along with the hawks which sometimes wheeled high over the house just as one was doing now.

'What a sight!' said Daniel, watching the bird through binoculars.

'We'd get a better view from the grounds,' mumbled Steve.

Daniel handed his brother the field-glasses. 'What *are* we going to do?'

'I've been thinking about it,' said Steve. He trained the glasses on the estate's boundary wall and followed it first up the hill to where it disappeared behind bracken, and then down to the point where it was lost in trees. 'There must be a way through or over that wall. If we can find a way in we can get down to the house and try to speak to the Laird. I'm sure he'll say everything's all right. It'll probably turn out that old McAllister is just having a mean turn. I expect he does it all the time, just so he can keep people out of his grounds.'

'And what if he catches us?'

'We make sure he doesn't.'

'But what if he does? You know how he sneaked up on us down at the lodge.'

'I dunno,' said Steve. 'Come on, let's have something to eat. I'm starving.'

They woke early next morning and crawled out of their tent into crisp, pale sunlight. 'It's going to be a crackin' day,' Daniel declared as they strolled down to the farmhouse to buy eggs. 'No more rain. I reckon we're in for a scorcher.'

It seemed he could be right; by the time they'd cleared away their breakfast things and started out towards the estate the sun was hot on their backs. And when they reached the old stone wall their faces were flushed and perspiring. Frustration made them hotter still. The wall was higher here than they had imagined and its tightly-fitting stones made it impossible to scale.

'But there must be *some* way in,' groaned Daniel after they had searched for half an hour – and eventually there was. Higher up the hill they found a breach where the roots of a tree had come up and disturbed the stone blocks and tumbled them out of place, leaving a gap just big enough for the boys to wriggle through. From there it was a simple matter of heading down through the pine forest towards the house.

Half-way there the trees thinned out and there was a break in the vegetation before dense shrubbery took over. This was not as high as the trees and for the first time the boys could look out over the estate at close quarters. They could see the house clearly, about two hundred metres away, and so they paused to use the binoculars, hoping to catch a glimpse of the Laird at one of the windows.

After a couple of minutes, though, Steve gave up and handed the glasses to Daniel. And Daniel was about to give up too when – 'Here, who's that? There's a girl at one of the windows.' He passed the glasses back. 'In that tower. Look!'

Steve looked. 'I can't see anyone,' he said flatly.

'She must have moved away. A girl with dark hair. Came to the window and stood there looking out.'

Steve lowered the glasses. 'You're not having me on?'

'Straight up – she was about fourteen.'

'If you say so. Anyway, it doesn't matter – it's the Laird we want. Come on.'

They went on down through the bushes, treading

softly and moving slowly so as not to alarm any birds or animals and give themselves away, and soon they were peering through the last stretch of shrubbery on the edge of the broad lawns that surrounded the rambling old house.

'What now?' Daniel asked in a low voice.

'We wait,' said Steve. 'We wait until we know where McAllister is, and until we're sure we can reach the Laird without anyone interfering.'

'Can't we just run up to the front door and knock?'

'And supposing McAllister answers it? For all we know he might be in there with the old boy right now. No, we need to be sure we can speak to the Laird.'

'All right. How about if I creep round to the back of the house, then, in case he's in a room round there?'

'Good idea. But make sure you keep well into the bushes. And don't make any noise.'

Daniel nodded and started off, but he had not gone twenty paces before he turned and called back to Steve in a loud whisper. 'Hey, look at this.'

His brother signalled desperately to him to keep quiet. Then he saw that Daniel was looking at something on the ground. He went over to him and found that it was a white trainer shoe wedged under a trailing root. 'Just an old shoe,' he said.

'Hardly old,' Daniel remarked. 'And look, it's got stuck under this root as though someone got it caught and their foot came out. See, the lace is still tied.'

'So what?' said Steve irritably. 'Does it matter to us?'

Daniel squatted down. 'Well, I dunno. Look here, the ground's all churned up as though someone fell.'

'I'm not surprised, if they got their foot caught under that root.'

Daniel wasn't listening. 'D.P.' he said.

'What?'

'The initials inside the shoe. D.P.'

Steve stared at his brother, a bit annoyed. 'Daniel, we're here to sort out our holiday, not to worry about lost shoes. And another thing — '

'*Oi! Who's there?*' The gruff voice sprang at them across the lawn.

'Heck, it's McAllister!' hissed Steve. 'Run for it!'

They sprinted back up through the shrubbery with more shouts ringing in their ears, feeling quite convinced that the gamekeeper was on their tail, but by the time they had reached the pine-woods and paused for breath they could hear no sound of pursuit.

'It's all right,' gasped Daniel. 'He's too heavy to run fast. He's given up.'

'It's not all right,' Steven retorted. 'If you hadn't been so interested in that shoe we would have seen him coming and kept quiet. Now he'll be on the lookout for us and we probably won't even have a chance to reach the Laird.'

Daniel muttered something in return and then they turned and ran on, slower this time, until they reached the hole in the wall and squeezed through. On the other side another Scottish voice growled at them — 'What are you boys up to?' — but after their hearts had nearly stopped they looked up with relief to see Alex grinning down at them.

'Don't *do* that, Alex!' Steve exploded. 'We just had a close shave with McAllister.'

The boy laughed. 'I told you he'd eat you for breakfast!'

'Don't joke,' said Daniel. 'Anyway, what are you doing up here?'

Alex told them that he had come up to the church with his father and called in to the farm for some milk. 'I saw the tent in the field and Mr Andrews said it belonged to a couple of English lads. I guessed it was you when he said you'd gone off exploring over here, so I've been sitting here waiting. Now what's all this about McAllister? And why aren't you camping in Hawk-towers like you said?'

'We'll tell you about it in a minute,' said Steve, wiping his perspiring face. 'But first let's find somewhere cool to sit.'

'You'd better come over to the church,' said Alex. 'It's always cool in there, even on the hottest day.'

And so they told Alex their story sitting in the chilly coolness of the solid old church and staring round at the bright stained-glass windows. It was a strange setting for their tale, Steve felt, and the atmosphere, along with the creaking of roof timbers expanding beneath the sun's heat, seemed to add a slightly eerie edge to his words.

Daniel, on the other hand, found the place somehow reassuring. It was a place of — what was the word? — *sanctuary*. There was a sort of security about the solid walls, he thought, and in the quiet moments when none of them was speaking he was aware of the friendly silence that hung on the cool air. It was as though someone was listening . . . waiting for him to whisper his secrets and to share the things that were bothering him. That shoe was bothering him . . . and that girl at the window. He didn't even know why. And then there were the osprey eggs . . .

As far as he could recall, he'd never prayed before in his entire life . . .

'What are you going to do now?' Alex asked, breaking the silence.

'I don't know,' Steve replied. 'I don't suppose your father would help us, would he? Do you think he'd have a word with the Laird for us?'

Alex shrugged. 'He might. But it'll have to wait. He's got a lot of paperwork to get through at the moment, out in his office.'

'That's all right. It's not as though we're desperate for

somewhere to camp, thanks to the farmer. But we really would like to get things sorted out with the Laird.'

'And with McAllister,' added Daniel. 'I'd feel a lot better if I knew that man was on my side.'

Alex grinned. 'Well, there's not much we can do now. Why don't you let me show you round the village? You can pick up any supplies you need at the same time.'

It was just as Alex had described – a quaint old Scottish fishing village with higgledy-piggledy houses and shops set on hilly streets, all leading down to the quiet harbour where working boats jostled each other on a rippling tide and the gulls hovered and swooped for a scrap of fish on the worn decks.

The brothers loved it; in fact they spent so much time exploring the old village that they quite forgot about the supplies they needed to buy and Alex had to remind them. 'Come on,' he said, 'I'll show you McFadden's – you'll get everything you want there. And while you're buying your things I'll slip along to the post office. I have to get some stamps for my father.'

McFadden's, they discovered, was one of those jumbly country stores that sold just about everything – groceries, newspapers, stationery, toys, clothing, fishing gear, ironmongery – and all packed into an amazingly small space.

'Like Aladdin's cave!' remarked Steve.

'Full of surprises,' added Daniel as his eyes fell on a range of pocket-knives. But the biggest surprise of them all leapt out from the front page of a newspaper on the counter.

'Steve, that's the girl!'

'What?'

Daniel glanced round to make sure no one was listening. 'Look,' he said, 'this picture in the paper – that's the girl I saw at the window in the old house.'

Steve studied the photograph of a teenage girl with

dark hair and smiling eyes. She was wearing a light-coloured sweater. He looked at his brother uncertainly. 'You're not having me on?'

'Course not! Would I joke about a thing like this?'

Steve picked up the paper and both boys read the report. It was about the kidnapped girl mentioned on the car radio the day before. Her name was Davina Phillips and she'd been abducted two miles from her school near the Cumbria coast four days ago. Her father, one of the wealthiest men in the country, had been given until noon the following day to hand over a ransom of two million pounds or he would never see his daughter again. The police had little idea where the girl was being held but believed she was still in the county. Apparently the alarm had been raised very soon after the abductors had struck and all roads out of the area had been sealed off.

Steve shook his head. 'You must be mistaken. They had road-blocks all over the place; they couldn't have got the girl this far north. Anyway, it's a crazy idea – you don't think the Laird would have anything to do with a thing like this, do you? For a start, he wouldn't have said we could camp in the grounds if he was planning a kidnapping, would he?'

'Well, I dunno – I suppose not,' Daniel admitted. 'But what about McAllister? He's mad enough to try it! And that would explain why he wanted to get rid of us, too!'

Steve wasn't convinced. 'You're letting your imagination run away with you. First a girl at the window, then an old shoe . . .'

'The shoe!' Suddenly Daniel's mind was racing. 'Steve, I've just remembered – *the initials*! There were initials in that trainer, remember – D.P.'

He snatched the paper from his brother's hands and scanned the report. 'There – Davina Phillips – D.P.! I'm *not* imagining it, Steve!'

Steve couldn't ignore that. He hadn't seen the girl at the window, but he'd certainly seen the lost trainer and those initials had been clearly marked. Yet it still didn't seem possible somehow. 'I admit it seems more than a coincidence, but − '

'And don't forget those marks on the ground,' Daniel cut in. 'They could have been made in a struggle. The girl probably tried to escape and they caught her just there − that's how her shoe came off!'

Steve thought about it. 'Look, we'll tell everything to Alex and see what he makes of it. If he thinks there's anything fishy we'll go to the police − all right?'

Daniel nodded. 'We'd better buy this paper and take it with us. And let's get the rest of the things we need as quickly as we can.'

They met Alex outside the store, just as they were leaving with their supplies. 'Looks like you bought the stock!' the boy laughed.

'Listen,' said Steve. 'We've got something to tell you. Go on, Daniel.'

The boy glanced around and was about to begin when his eyes almost jumped out of his head. 'Oh, heck − it's him!'

The others followed his gaze. 'Who?' asked Alex. 'What's going on?'

'Down there on the harbour, by the Land-Rover. It's McAllister, see? There − talking with that bloke on the cruiser. We'd better not let him see us.'

Alex glanced at the man, then back at Daniel. 'But that's not McAllister.'

The brothers stared. 'It's *not*? Are you sure?'

'Of course I'm sure.'

'But he's the one who kicked us out of Hawktowers.'

The young Scot shrugged. 'Maybe they've taken on an assistant gamekeeper.'

Daniel ignored this. He turned to his brother. 'Steve,

that would explain about the osprey eggs – why he didn't know they'd already hatched!'

Steve agreed. 'But where's the real McAllister? And the Laird?'

'Probably tied up somewhere in the old house. Down in the cellar, maybe.'

'If they're still alive.'

Alex could hardly believe his ears. 'Look, would someone please tell me what's going on?'

'Sorry,' said Daniel, 'but we've just worked it out. You see, that bloke we thought was McAllister isn't a gamekeeper at all. He's a criminal – a kidnapper, actually.'

Alex laughed. 'Och, is this a joke?'

'I'm afraid not,' said Steve, his voice deadly serious. He thrust the newspaper into the boy's hands. 'Here, read this. Then we want you to show us where the police station is – and quick!'

There was no police station in the village; only a police house at the top of the hill. So, after the brothers had told Alex all they knew, they started up the narrow street. But they had not gone far when they heard a Land-Rover behind them, and with a glance over their shoulders their hearts began to race. It was coming for them!

'In here!' gasped Steve, quickly steering the others into an alleyway. There they flung themselves against a wall and stood trembling in the late afternoon shadows as the growling of the vehicle drew nearer.

'C-can't we run for it?' gasped Daniel.

'No use!' retorted Alex. 'This is a dead end!'

Steve set down the box of supplies in case he was going to have to fight, and in a cold sweat he heard the Land-Rover slow and change gear. They were in for it now!

There was a sudden echoing roar as the vehicle passed the alleyway . . . and kept going!

The boys almost collapsed with relief.

'Did you see?' said Alex. 'They were both in the cab – your gamekeeper and the fellow from the boat. Probably going to get the girl.'

'What?' said Steve.

They stepped into the street as the Land-Rover disappeared round a bend. 'Well, it's obvious, isn't it? They're all part of the gang. They used the cruiser to get the girl out of the area – to bring her up here where no one would ever think of looking for her.'

'Of course!' Daniel's eyes flashed with excitement. 'They knew the police would seal off the roads, but as the school was only a few miles from the coast they had the perfect getaway.'

'And the perfect hiding place, too,' said Steve. 'Hawktowers – miles from anywhere!'

'And now they're getting ready to move her again,' Alex went on. 'Probably to release her once the ransom's handed over.'

'*If* they intend to release her,' said Steve, shivering at his own thought.

Alex ignored him and reached for the newspaper. 'When's the deadline?'

'Noon tomorrow,' said Daniel.

Alex scanned the report again. 'So that means they'll probably plan to move her tonight, under cover of darkness.'

Steve glanced at his watch. 'It's almost six now – only a few hours of daylight left. Come on, to the police house – quick!'

The local constabulary answered a knock at the door in shirt-sleeves and braces, and with a serviette tucked into the neck of its shirt. He was a tall, stocky man with a ruddy face and a scowl. 'I'm off duty,' he said quickly, eyeing the boys up and down. 'What is it, young Alex? Make it quick because I'm in the middle of my tea.'

24

'Sergeant Galley, it's about the kidnapped girl,' the boy began. 'They've got her at Hawktowers and we think they're going to move her in that boat down there tonight.'

The officer blinked. 'What? Is this some sort of foolishness?'

Alex started again, telling the whole story, with Steve and Daniel chipping in with bits he left out, but it was a rushed and jumbled account and not very convincing to a hungry man whose sausages were getting cold on his plate.

'Look,' he said irritably, 'there's probably a perfectly reasonable explanation for all of this. For a start Mr McAllister usually takes a holiday about this time of year. The man you saw is almost certainly standing in for him – and if you were anything of a Sherlock Holmes you'd have discovered that for yourselves. As for a girl at the window – well, it might well be the Laird's grand-daughter. He's got three, did you know that? And the boat – ' he glanced down to the harbour below where evening sunlight picked out the bright white of the cabin-cruiser – 'there's no law against a gamekeeper having a friend with a boat. Now why don't you run along and let me finish my tea?'

'But the shoe with the initials – '

The sergeant shrugged. 'Coincidence, I dare say.'

'But we *know* it's the girl,' pleaded Steve. 'You *must* do something!'

'You're right,' rasped the sergeant. 'I *must* finish my tea. Now go away and annoy someone else.'

He went in and shut the door with a bang and the boys turned to face one another. 'Rats!' said Daniel. 'I thought he'd jump at the chance of being a hero. He could get his name in the papers!'

'At least he could have reported it for us,' grumbled Steve.

'So what do we do now?' asked Alex.

'Would your father help?' said Daniel.

'If he believed it really was the girl, yes. The trouble is, I don't think anyone *will* believe us.'

'In that case there's only one thing we can do,' Daniel decided. 'We must rescue the girl ourselves.'

'And how are we going to do that?' Steve scoffed.

Daniel felt strangely optimistic. 'I dunno. But we'll think of something.'

They knew they had to act fast and that they would get only one chance at getting the girl out. If anything went wrong − well, then they would find out just how desperate these men were. But they had to try. And by the time they reached the farm they had a plan. All it needed was good timing, a suitable diversion, a hammer and a length of rope. They already had a hammer − the one they used for the tent-pegs − and they found a rope in the farmer's barn. Then they were off across the road, through the hole in the wall, and down through the trees towards the house. By the time they reached the last line of bushes it was fully dusk. Curtains had been drawn at the window where Daniel had spied the girl and a soft light shone behind them.

'Looks like she's still there,' whispered Daniel, 'but we'd better check, just in case.' He stooped and picked some small stones from the earth. 'Boy, I wish I had a catapult.'

In the shadows of the early evening he stood in a break between two bushes and flung first one stone and then another at the window. Both fell short. A third, heavier stone struck the glass but it drew no response. He waited a few seconds then threw again. Another strike. This time the curtain was pulled aside and the girl was there, peering out into the gathering gloom, looking this way and that as she scanned the dark gardens. After half a minute she went away.

'Right,' Steve said softly, 'now we need to work out the diversion.'

They had already agreed that this should be Alex's job; he had been here on two occasions and knew the layout on the other side of the house. There was an old barn and a workshop, he remembered, and he was sure he could find something that could be used to distract the gang while the others got the girl out.

'Go and have a scout round,' said Daniel. 'Then report back and let us know what you've found.'

Alex nodded and went off through the darkness, leaving the brothers to finalize their plans for the rescue. They had already decided that one of them would climb the drainpipe running up by the girl's window and then smash the glass with the hammer. 'But we'd better get the girl to put a pillow up to the window,' said Daniel. 'That'll deaden the noise of splintering glass.'

The rope would be used for the getaway. It wasn't enough to trust the drainpipe, they decided; it looked too rickety to bear a lot of scrambling up and down it, and the girl might not be too clever at escaping that way. If she fell and busted a leg they'd be in trouble.

'So who's going to get her out?' asked Steve.

'It'd better be you,' said Daniel. 'You're lighter, and you're good at gymnastics, too. I'd probably fall off the bloomin' drainpipe.'

'Terrific,' hissed Steve. 'You get the ideas and I get the dangerous bit.'

Just then there was a rustling in the bushes and their hearts leapt in panic. But it was only Alex returning.

'Find anything?' Daniel asked.

The boy gave a 'thumbs up'. 'There's a bench-saw in the workshop and a couple of motor-mowers in the barn. They're all in good shape so I'd expect them to start easily. Together they'll make quite a row. Oh, and by the way, the Land-Rover's round there.'

'OK,' said Steve. 'That probably means they're all in the house. Watch out for the mad gamekeeper!' He turned to Daniel. 'You'll have to watch the house and give Alex the signal to start up the motors – use a bird-call – and as soon as he gets that going I'll break the glass. But for Pete's sake don't whistle till you know I'm in position outside the window. OK?'

'OK.'

'Right, let's do it. And good luck.'

'I think we'll need more than luck,' said Daniel. 'I've been praying like mad. I just wish we weren't on our own.'

'Well, we're not,' smiled Alex. 'Not if you've been praying.' He turned to go, then looked back at Daniel. 'Make that three bird-calls with five seconds between each one, just so as I'll know it's you.'

'Three calls,' Daniel repeated.

Steve said, 'I'd better go too.'

'Hang on,' said Daniel, and he got down and felt about under one of the bushes. He came up again with a trainer in his hand. 'She'll need this.'

Steve tucked the shoe into his belt and adjusted the coil of rope over his shoulder. Finally he checked the hammer hanging at his side, stuck his head out of the bush to check for sounds, and then he was gone, flitting silently across the dark lawn like a shadow.

From the cover of the shrubbery Daniel watched him disappear into the darkness around the house, then reappear halfway up the drainpipe a minute later. Soon he was at the window and tapped gently on the glass. Almost instantly the curtains parted and the girl stood staring at him, alarmed for only a second before she realized what was happening. Though the main window had been securely locked there was a small fanlight at the top and she opened it immediately so that she could hear what Steve was trying to say to her.

'We'll soon have you out,' he whispered. 'Bring a pillow and put it up against the glass.'

Down below Daniel watched as Steve brought up the hammer and the girl put the pillow in place. *Phreeep*. He gave the first whistle. *Phreeep*. Five seconds. *Phreeep*.

On the other side of the house in the workshop Alex threw the switch on the electric saw, then ran to the barn and started up the mowers, throwing them into motion so that they went clattering out of the barn on to the stone chippings of the drive.

Steve brought back the hammer and smacked it on the glass. *Nothing happened!* He struck again, harder this time. The hammer just bounced!

Daniel watched nervously as lights came on at the front of the house and someone started shouting inside. Then the main doors were flung open and two men came running out, heading for the barn. Had Alex got away all right?

The hammer whacked into the glass again – *crash!* At last!

But instantly another noise joined the row. *Alarm bells!*

Daniel could have kicked himself. Why hadn't they thought of the burglar alarm?

Fighting panic, Steve thrust the end of the rope into the girl's hands. 'Loop it under the leg of the bed!' he shouted. It didn't matter how much noise he made now. 'Hurry!'

There was no time for the shoe. He let out the rest of the rope. 'Follow me down – and mind yourself on this jagged glass!'

He slid down the rope, burning his hands as he went, and seconds later the girl followed, jumping the last few feet so that she caught Steve's shoulder and they both went down. Scrambling to their feet, they started across the lawn, and suddenly Daniel was out in the open, shouting, 'Move it, Steve! They're coming!'

Heavy boots came pounding on gravel from the back of the house. 'There they are!'

'Down the drive!' bawled Daniel. 'Our best chance!'

He ran to meet them and grabbed one of the girl's hands. 'Run for it!'

Steve caught her other hand and together the brothers raced with her across the grass down through the avenue of trees that would lead them to the main gate.

'What happened to Alex?' Steve gasped.

'Dunno! Maybe they got him!'

Blam! A shotgun blast went over their heads. 'Hold it or I'll let you have the other barrel!'

It was the mad gamekeeper and he was chasing them, chasing them hard.

'He means it!' trembled Steve.

They slowed to a halt and turned, panting and shaking. Daniel glanced at the girl. 'Sorry.'

She smiled sadly. 'Thanks for trying. Both of you.'

Steve handed her the trainer. 'You might as well put this on now.'

'Back to the house!' barked the gunman. 'And no tricks!'

In the bright light that shone out from the front of the house they could see that they had got Alex, too. He was shouting and kicking as one of the men dragged him across the drive, but it was no use.

'Well, that's it,' said Steve. 'Now we've *all* had it.'

'Police! Drop the gun!' The stern command rang out from the bushes and the gamekeeper swung round as powerful lights flashed on, dazzling him. At the same time half a dozen marksmen broke cover and held him in their rifle sights.

Steve gave a whoop of delight. 'The police! How did they get here?'

But it wasn't over yet. The man dragging Alex – the man from the boat – hooked his arm round the boy's

30

neck and started backing away towards the Land-Rover. 'If you shoot you'll hit the kid,' he yelled, and then he was thrusting Alex into the cab and climbing in behind. The engine fired and roared, tyres spinning, and the vehicle shot away down the drive.

'Hold your fire!' shouted the police officer.

In the cab Alex wriggled and fought, grabbing at the steering-wheel, stamping on the driver's foot, biting his arm — but one blow sent the boy crashing across the seat and out of the passenger door. The boys watched him fall, tumbling out on to the grass, but he seemed to bounce right up again. 'Good ol' Alex!' they cheered.

The Land-Rover charged on, belting down the drive and away — but its flight was short-lived. Police sirens filled the air and headlights flashed through the main gate. The boys counted one, two, three . . . six cars!

'Here comes the cavalry!' cried Daniel. 'They've got him trapped!'

With tyres screaming, the cars fanned out across the drive and lawns, blocking any chance of escape — and forcing the Land-Rover towards the trees . . . and into a ditch!

'Got him!' laughed Steve. 'And serves him right!'

Back at the house the third member of the gang snarled his rage at the gamekeeper as police officers forced their arms behind their backs and snapped on the hand-cuffs. 'Beaten by a bunch of kids! I told yer — yer should've done 'em in when they first come snoopin' round the place.'

The bogus McAllister said nothing as he was led away — just glared fiercely at them.

Alex came up the drive, rubbing his elbow, and a police car drew alongside. 'Are you all right, son?'

'Dad! What are you doing here?'

The vicar raised an eyebrow. 'I might ask you the same thing.'

Beside him, in the back seat of the car, Sergeant Galley leaned forward. 'It's thanks to your father that we're here at all, laddie.'

Inside the house, seated in the library with cups of hot chocolate to warm them, they heard how Alex's father had called at the police house on parish business and learned about the three lads interrupting the constabulary tea with their wild story. 'I thought it all a bit of a joke,' the sergeant admitted, 'but then the vicar here told me he'd seen McAllister's Land-Rover on the harbour last Tuesday evening – the same day the girl was abducted.'

'Aye, and two men were moving something from the boat to the back of the Land-Rover,' the vicar went on. 'Something that from a distance looked like a roll of carpet – but what we now know was Davina here.'

The girl smiled and the sergeant looked faintly embarrassed. 'Er, well – naturally, when I heard about that I had to reconsider your report, lads, so I made enquiries about the boat – the *Sea Dream* – and discovered that it was on hire to a certain Mr Felix Baxter.'

'The Laird's nephew!' exclaimed Alex.

'Aye. And as he had a police record of robbery and fraud it very quickly became apparent that you boys had got it right. We didn't hang about after that. One telephone call to area headquarters and things moved pretty fast from then on.' He hesitated. 'I - er – I owe you lads an apology.'

'That's all right,' said Steve. 'We're just glad you came when you did. It might have been a very different ending but for that.'

'You know, it's funny,' said Daniel, 'but I somehow knew it would end up all right, even when McAllister had the drop on us. It sounds crazy, I know, but something seemed to tell me it would be OK.'

'That's not so crazy,' said Alex's father. 'Though I'd rather say some*one* . . .'

'Well, I did say a sort of prayer about all this — before things really started to happen, that is.'

Steve was surprised. 'Did you? When?'

'This morning, in the church. It was so lovely and peaceful in there, and yet I couldn't stop thinking about the face at the window, and about the shoe. It was worrying me for some reason. I suppose I couldn't help feeling that something was wrong — so I just asked God if he would sort it out. And I wasn't worried after that. Funny, isn't it?'

Alex was about to say something when the door to the library opened and a police inspector brought in an old man in a crumpled tweed suit and carpet slippers. No one needed to tell them that it was the Laird. He had a big friendly face topped with a shock of white hair. Behind him came a taller figure, much younger and of a strong build. His clothes told the boys that this was McAllister — the real one! Both men looked tired, but they smiled a great deal as they were introduced to the lads — and Davina Phillips. They had not seen her before; in fact they'd had no idea what the Laird's villainous nephew was up to. The gang had kept them locked in the cellars since the day before the kidnapping.

'But mercifully that's all over now — thanks to you boys,' said the Laird. 'We're deeply grateful to you.' He turned to the girl. 'Aren't we, my dear?'

Davina grinned, shyly tossing back her dark hair. 'There'll probably be a reward of some sort. Daddy will want to thank you somehow, I'm sure.'

The three lads shrugged self-consciously, and Steve said, 'All we really want is our holiday here at Hawktowers — to study the animals and birds.'

'And you shall have it,' said the Laird. 'You shall have the best room in the house for as long as you wish.'

33

'And I'll show you the best places for observing the wildlife here on the estate,' added McAllister. 'Just let me know what you want to see and I'll arrange it.'

'Wow!' exclaimed Steve. 'A guided tour! That's more than we ever could have hoped for!'

Just then a constable appeared at the door and looked to the inspector. 'May I have a word, sir?'

'What is it, Foster?'

'The girl's parents, sir. We've been in touch and they're on their way.'

For the first time the girl cried.

The following morning, after an idyllic calm had returned to Hawktowers, three young lads strolled quietly through the grounds with the Laird and his gamekeeper. There was little trace of the drama that had exploded around the country estate only hours earlier, and already the boys had put the adventure behind them. The only thing that captivated them now was observing the wildlife that had brought the two brothers to Scotland, to Hawktowers with its growing reputation as a haven for threatened species. The lads said as much to the Laird as they came down through the shrubbery and on to the lawns, and the old boy laughed. 'Felt a bit like a threatened species myself over the last few days,' he chortled. 'But you didn't come all this way to observe a nutty old man – I think *that's* more what you had in mind, up there.'

The boys looked skyward, and gasped. '*The ospreys!*' The rare, magnificent birds were wheeling high over the trout stream, gently riding the currents in a sky of crystal blue.

'They're looking for fish,' said Steve, tracking the birds with the binoculars. 'He'll dive any minute!'

They watched, spellbound, as one of the birds dropped its height until it was flapping and gliding at about sixty feet above the shimmering water. Then, with wings half-closed, it plummeted towards the surface, claws outstretched, splashing spectacularly into the currents . . . and rose high into the air again, a huge silver fish as its prize!

'Fantastic!' exclaimed Steve.

'Beautiful birds, aren't they?' said the Laird. 'We're very privileged that they return here year after year.'

'It's a good thing they do,' said Daniel. 'After all, it was the ospreys that first made us think something was wrong at Hawktowers. It was the eggs, you see.'

'Eggs?' said the Laird. 'But there aren't any osprey eggs now – isn't that so, McAllister?'

The gamekeeper nodded. 'Quite right, sir. Hatched weeks ago, at the beginning of June.'

Daniel watched as the osprey joined its mate and the two of them moved away into the cover of the trees. 'Ah,' he said, 'but not everyone knows that. Not even some gamekeepers . . .'

Sheriff Morgan's Showdown

One thing's for sure, young Tom ain't likely to forget how it began. At the time he and Chuck were out at Broken Creek tryin' for the hundredth time to coax that big ol' catfish to swallow the hook on the end of their line, and Tom swears he near as had him. It was then Chuck missed his footin' and landed in the water . . . and the fish vamoosed.

As if the day wasn't hot enough, Tom threw down his hickory rod and began calling his buddy some names that just about set the afternoon air on fire.

'I − I couldn't help it,' Chuck moaned as he climbed back on to the bank, drippin' wet. 'I was watching them fellers.'

'*What* fellers?' roared Tom, and then he looked up to see 'em riding by. He didn't say no more. Just gave a sort o' strangled gulp.

There were three of 'em and it was a real contest to know which looked the meanest: the one in black with the silver pistols; the scruffy one with the scars and the shotgun; or the slit-eyed Mexican with the long-bladed knife strapped to his boot. Why, they was mean enough to just *look* someone to death, and Tom said so.

'Th-they're headin' for town!' stammered Chuck, explaining why he'd ruined the fishing. 'And with all them guns!'

Tom looked at his buddy with wide eyes. 'You reckon they're lookin' for trouble?'

The strangers were away down the trail by now so Chuck figured he could speak his mind. 'Well, they sure ain't headin' for no picnic. Come on, let's get back. We sure as heck don't wanna miss anythin'. And I'll bet ya there's gonna be sparks when the Sheriff tries to take their guns.'

Now this was a new ruling in Jarrettville, and seeing as the town had grown some and there were often strangers passing through it seemed like a useful law to have visitors deposit their firearms at the Sheriff's office while in town. Normally, of course, this presented no problem since most folks were keen to help keep the peace, but now and then some ornery cowboy would have a difference of opinion with Sheriff Morgan and there'd be some hot lead flyin' around. Such a happening seemed a distinct possibility with them three jackals headin' for town and the boys weren't figuring to hear about it second-hand. They ran like their tails were on fire to make sure they didn't have to.

When they came steamin' round the last corner and into the main street they knew they were in time. The Sheriff had caught the strangers just as they were about to slip into the hotel and now he was sayin' his piece.

'Come on,' Chuck urged, 'we can come around from behind and sneak under the boardwalk. We can get real close under there.'

That was a pretty smart idea. The boys would be out of harm's way beneath the boards of the raised walkway, and from there they'd hear every word of the confrontation. They'd see the action, too, if they lifted that loose board.

'But that's the ruling here, boys,' the Sheriff was saying as Tom and Chuck started wriggling into position. 'No guns to be worn or carried in town. Either you hand 'em over or I'll ask you to leave.'

'No,' said the Mexican. 'We keep the guns *and* we stay. That is *our* ruling. But eef you wanna fight about it — '

37

Lying in the cool dust beneath the boards the boys felt a shiver chase down their spines. Yessir, there was gonna be trouble.

But their excitement turned out to be a shade premature. For crossin' the street at that moment, and looking determined to make the incident his own business, came the black-clad figure of the Rev. Silas T. Holliman, a preacher who had stopped off in Jarrettville for a few days to break his journey through Wyoming. Word had it that he was on his way to take up a new church somewheres down in Colorado. Tom and Chuck knew all o' this and more since Tom's pa ran the livery stable and there wasn't no coming or going in this town without Tom hearing about it over the supper table. The boys reckoned that was a real useful source of information, since there was nothing about the man's appearance which suggested his profession – not even the big ol' Bible most preachers carried – and they might just have made the mistake of getting talking to the Rev. Holliman in the street and found themselves in for a sudden sermon. That would have been too bad. Long ago they'd decided that preachers, like school-ma'ams, were best avoided lest they try to sneak in an extra bit of teachin' while you're not lookin'! Doggone it, there was a limit to how much learnin' a youngster could bear!

But it didn't look like the Reverend was fixing to deliver no sermon, and from their worm's-eye view the boys suddenly began to look up to the preacher with a new interest.

'Can I be of help, Sheriff?' he called across the street. 'I believe I detect a difference of opinion.'

'Nothing I can't handle, Mr Holliman,' the Sheriff replied. 'These gents were just about to comply with the town's ruling about guns being carried in town.'

'And wisely so,' said the Reverend. 'Every man has a

duty to uphold the laws of – '

'Keep out of this, preacher,' growled Scar-face. 'We don't need no pulpit lesson.'

'I'm sure not, sir,' the preacher smiled. 'In fact, I'm sure you'll see reason and do as the Sheriff here asks.'

Now that was a tricky moment and it went so quiet that Tom was sure he could have cut the air with the Mexican's knife. Any second he expected to hear the men back off and start hurlin' lead. But to the boys' surprise it never came to that.

It was then that the silver pistols spoke up. 'I'll tell you what we'll do, Reverend. We'll hand over our irons if this heap o' dirt with the badge asks us real nice.'

Beneath the boards the boys held their breath. That fella was just askin' for a showdown. But Tom and Chuck were in for another surprise.

'All right,' they heard Sheriff Morgan say, and he sounded as sweet as Miss Wimple's apple pie. 'Would you boys kindly hand over your guns . . . please?'

Chuck's mouth fell open and Tom blinked hard. Were they hearing right?

Then a burst of mockin' laughter filled their ears and the strangers removed their pistols and handed them over. Scar-face tossed his shotgun into the Sheriff's arms, too.

'Another time, maybe,' snarled the Mexican, and with that the three of 'em headed into the hotel.

'Well, how d'you like that!' hissed Chuck. 'We done been cheated out of any action.' And with that he went wriggling out into the street. Tom was right behind him.

'Well, well,' said the Sheriff's voice from above. 'If it ain't a pair o' sidewinders slithering through the dirt! How long you boys been under there?'

Chuck jumped to his feet and stood smackin' the dust out of his pants. 'Long enough to hear everything, Sheriff – but now I wish we hadn't heard nothin' at all.'

'Oh? Why's that?'

Tom got to his feet beside his buddy and pulled the face he usually reserved for his ma's spinach pie. 'How could you let them fellers talk to you like that, J.J.? We was expectin' a showdown.'

Sheriff J. J. Morgan laughed and pushed back his wide-brimmed hat. 'Well now, you don't expect me to shoot it out with every stranger that rides into town, do you?'

'No sir,' said Tom, 'but I don't see why you had to be so accommodatin' to them fellers, neither – calling you a heap o' dirt an' all.'

'Well, that's a little trick I learned, Tom,' the Sheriff explained. 'A way o' disarmin' tricky troublemakers without having to squeeze off a single shot.'

The boys stared. 'Huh?'

'It's simple,' said J.J. 'Something I read in the Good Book – "A soft answer turneth away wrath". You ever hear that?'

The boys shook their heads. They weren't too familiar with the Bible.

J.J. smiled as he reached inside his jacket and pulled out the chunky little book he liked to carry around with him. Then he opened it up and showed the boys where them words were found. 'A soft answer turneth away wrath,' he said again. 'Proverbs chapter fifteen, verse one.'

The boys nodded politely, hoping this wasn't going to take long.

'You wanna read some more?' the Sheriff asked, offering them the black-bound book.

'Er – no sir,' said Chuck. 'Not right now.'

'Pity,' said the lawman. 'Y'know, you boys really oughtta make friends with the Bible – you never can tell when it might save your hide.' And with that he turned and went about his business, leaving them youngsters wondering what to say.

'I'll never figure him,' said Tom as they headed across the street. 'Bibles are for preachers and Sunday sermons. Don't seem natural for a gunslinger to have such a likin' for that old book.'

'Hush,' said Chuck, and he gave an anxious glance over his shoulder. 'J.J. mighta been a gunslinger once, but he ain't now an' you know it.'

'Well, that takes some figurin', too,' Tom told him. 'Beats me how a man like that can change.'

Now, no one coulda blamed them boys for bein' a mite confused. After all, it ain't every day that a notorious gunfighter with a whole bunch o' notches on his gun suddenly swings around and starts protectin' people instead of shootin' 'em. But, as J.J. will tell you, there ain't nobody more surprised about it than he is.

It happened some while back, over in Banyon City. J.J. had only been in town an hour or two and was enjoying a quiet game o' cards in the Lucky Nugget saloon when he was called out to the street by the Firebrand Kid, a local no-good who fancied himself as the fastest gun in the county. The Kid also happened to think it would do his reputation no harm whatsoever if his shootin' could put the famous J. J. Morgan six feet under, and he wasn't shy about tellin' the world that this would be easier than fallin' off a greased log. Seems he figured J.J. was past it as a gunfighter and he was mighty keen to prove it — so much so that he started callin' Morgan some real unsociable names. Before the day was much older the two men were facin' each other down the main thoroughfare.

Now, J.J. had only two rules about gunfightin'. First, never start a fight. And second, never draw first. Abidin' by those principles had kept him out of prison all those years — legally speakin', every time he'd killed a man it had been in self-defence — and he wasn't aimin' to change things for the Firebrand Kid. When J. J. Morgan went for his long-barrelled Army Colt the Kid's pistol was clean out of its holster. But there the advantage changed. Those who were there say they never saw J.J.'s gun clear leather, but they sure heard the bark of that big ol' iron, and they wasn't in no doubt about the Kid's state o' health when he hit the ground, neither.

But, as J.J. found out, that trigger-happy boy wasn't all mouth. He got off one shot before J.J.'s Colt barked and that one slug just about made mashed potato of the gunfighter's left kneecap.

The result was that J.J. Morgan spent the next three months on his back in the Banyon City Hotel − an inconvenience that cost him every last cent he'd won in the Lucky Nugget that afternoon − but, as he now says, that was just about the best bit o' bad luck a man ever had. For it was while he was thus out of commission that he took to readin' everything he could lay his hands on, and when he'd got through every scrap o' newsprint in the city he took to thumbin' through an old Bible he found in his bedside cabinet. Truth is, the Good Book was the last thing the gunfighter wanted to read, but, as the man says, that book spoke to him louder than any six-shooter.

When he got off that bed eleven weeks later, J. J. Morgan was a changed man. Folks were suspicious at first, of course, but as he got around town, exercising that stiff leg o' his, they got to realizing that the man really was different. For a start he no longer packed that mean-lookin' pistol, and it seemed he couldn't do enough to help where help was needed. Started attending church, too, and one time he even stood up and told how the Good Lord had shaken him up and cleaned him out. 'Fact is, I feel like a new-born babe inside,' he told his hearers − and by that time there wasn't a soul in Banyon City didn't believe him. After that he became a real popular figure about town, and next thing people were calling for J.J. to be signed on as a peace officer.

Now, the truth is that if Banyon City hadn't already got its quota of lawmen, young Tom and Chuck would never have been so confused. As it was, the circuit judge had mentioned to J.J. that Jarrettville was looking to appoint a sheriff, and bein' in need of work – and knowing no other skill than how to shoot straight – he applied for the job.

At the time, the boys had greeted this news with glee and had gone about leapin' and whoopin' like a couple o' Red Injuns. As far as they was concerned the town was all too quiet and the prospect of a former gun-fighter as sheriff promised to liven things up a little. But, as it turned out, it seemed the boys were always in school when the sparks were flyin' and they'd missed all the fun. That was bad enough – but now, just as it looked like they was in for a showdown, Sheriff Morgan had backed down. Why, that was just too bad! As they headed over to Archie Duke's General Store to gaze at the candy-sticks they felt plumb cheated.

'It don't seem right that we should never get to see that fast draw o' his,' Chuck complained. 'And as for him always quotin' the Bible – well, that don't seem right, neither. Why, I declare he sounds more like a preacher than that preacher feller, Reverend Holliman. I ain't heard *him* speak one Bible text yet and that's a fact.'

'Well, he might just be about to,' said Tom. 'See there – he's on his way over to the Sheriff's place right now.'

They stood and watched as the Rev. Holliman crossed the street and stepped into the lawman's office. Then Chuck said, 'C'mon, Tom – them candy-sticks are callin' me somethin' powerful.'

Across the street it was the coffee that was calling Sheriff Morgan. 'Care to join me, Mr Holliman?' he asked as he poured himself a cup.

'Don't mind if I do,' the preacher replied. 'The dust of these little towns seems to get in my throat.'

J.J. passed his visitor a steaming mug. 'Sure, sure,' he said. Then − 'What's on your mind?'

'I came to apologize,' came the reply, 'in case you thought I was out of line, butting in while you were dealing with those rough-looking strangers.'

'I was only concerned for your safety, Reverend,' J.J. told him. 'Them sort o' fellers would shoot a man soon as look at him − and I dare say they wouldn't need much of an excuse. Could be they've got one on their mind, too.'

The preacher stared. 'Oh?'

'Got the payroll money for the ranches coming in tomorrow. That could be an awful big temptation to some men.'

'I see,' said the Reverend. 'You think those strangers are likely to make a play for it?'

The Sheriff smiled. 'Let's just say I'll feel a whole lot safer knowin' I've got their firearms under lock and key. This is a quiet little town, Reverend − I'd sure hate anything to change that.'

The Rev. Holliman sipped his coffee. 'Correct me if I'm wrong, Sheriff, but I seem to recall that Jarrettville wasn't so quiet about this time last year. Didn't you have some trouble here when that shipment of gold was stolen?'

'That's correct,' said J.J. 'The mining company's wagon was ambushed by a gang just a couple o' miles outside town and there was quite a shoot-out. Three guards were killed, along with every member of the gang 'cept one. He was the one made off with the gold − man by the name of Hogan, Wesley Hogan. They tracked him down next morning and found him hidin' out just the other side o' town. 'Course, by that time he'd hidden the gold.'

The Reverend shook his head. 'And no doubt he went to prison without telling where it was, and expecting to be rich when he got out.'

'I reckon that was his plan,' said J.J. 'The thing is, he took sick in his cell and died right there on his bunk.'

'Is that a fact?'

The Sheriff nodded. 'And the gold's still out there somewhere, probably buried in some hole in the ground. Could be it'll never be recovered now.'

The preacher set down his coffee mug. 'Well, who knows – maybe some needy soul will stumble upon it one day and get himself a fine reward. What does the Good Book say? "Seek and ye shall find"?'

'Book of Psalms,' remarked the Sheriff, 'if my memory serves me correctly.'

The Reverend nodded. 'Yes, "Seek and ye shall find".' You know, Sheriff, that might very well be my own personal text, seeing as my calling is to seek out life's lost and wandering souls. That's my first priority when I get to my new church, of course.'

'Of course.' J.J. sat back and finished his coffee. 'Y'know, Reverend, it's a pity you won't be staying on here through Sunday. We sure could use a preacher down at the church. Reverend Chiles – our circuit minister – he took sick this past week and it seems we're gonna be short of a sermon come the Sabbath.'

'I wish I could oblige, Sheriff,' the preacher remarked, 'but I really must be moving on just as soon as my horses are properly rested. Mind you, I'd appreciate the opportunity to look over your church building. I see it's quite a new place. In fact, I'd be glad if I could spend some time in there tomorrow, in prayer for my new calling – and for your own town, too, of course.'

The Sheriff smiled. 'Well, I'm sure that can be arranged. Why not call in and see Miss Bloom over at the drapery store? She holds the key and I'm sure it'll be in order for you to use the place.'

'Say, I'd appreciate that,' smiled the preacher.

'Stay all day, if you care to,' J.J. told him. 'No one'll disturb you there – unless, o' course, someone makes a play for that payroll money, in which case there'll be some shootin'. Maybe you'd better pray that won't happen.'

'I'll surely do that, Sheriff – you know, prayer is always such a good investment.'

With that the Rev. Holliman left, and Sheriff J. J. Morgan stood watching him go . . . wondering what the heck that feller was up to. He certainly wasn't all he seemed. J.J. figured he might find out more if he paid a visit to the livery stable.

The boys were there, horsin' around in the hay and suckin' on the candy-sticks Mr Duke had given them to get out of his store. (It wasn't that he disliked the youngsters, but he hated untidiness, and Tom and Chuck sure were the closest thing to untidiness in Jarrettville.)

'Your pa around, Tom?' the Sheriff called out.

The boy climbed out of the hay and came scrambling from under a horse. 'No sir, he's over with the blacksmith. You want me to go get 'im?'

'No, I guess I can find what I want without him. I'm lookin' for the preacher-man's wagon – is it around here?'

'Sure, it's out the back – but whaddya want with that?'

'Is he fixin' to leave?' asked Chuck as he stood there pullin' straw out of his hair.

J.J. knew how to handle these boys. Glancin' back towards the street, he stretched an arm round each of their shoulders and drew them closer together, lowering his voice. 'Now, boys, this is official business and I sure

46

could use your help.'

'Gee,' said Tom, 'y'mean you need a couple o' deputies?'

'You're dead right I do. I need a couple o' fellers I can trust — can I count on you?'

Suddenly them kids felt real important. 'Why, yessir,' answered Tom. 'Is there gonna be trouble?'

'Could be,' said the Sheriff, 'but right now I need to take a looksee inside that wagon, and I want you boys to keep an eye out in case the Reverend comes this way. Reckon you can handle that?'

'*Can* we?' said Chuck, his chest swellin' with pride. 'But what's it all about? Is the preacher in some kinda trouble?'

That was a tricky one. 'He might be, son. But right now I'm just curious to see what sort o' things he's carryin' around the country with him.'

Now it didn't take the Sheriff long to find out what he wanted to know, and he was back with Tom and Chuck before they knew it.

'Thanks, fellers, you did just fine.'

'What did you find out?' Chuck wanted to know.

'I can't tell you that right now,' the Sheriff said, 'and I don't want you boys sneakin' a look in that wagon, neither. But I appreciate your help.'

'Any time,' said Tom. 'This deputy work comes real easy to us, Sheriff.'

'I guess it does at that,' J.J. grinned. And then he was gone, headin' back up the street.

'Wow!' said Chuck, turning to his buddy. 'I never knew it felt so good to be a lawman.'

J.J., on the other hand, was feeling less than excited about wearing that tin star. In fact he was plumb worried. Somethin' ugly was about to happen in his town and he didn't like it. Worst of all, he knew he'd have to wait for things to start movin' before he could

47

act, and he wasn't used to that. Every gunfight he'd ever had had blown up and been settled within the hour, and it didn't suit him to have to sleep on it. But there were advantages, he decided, in having notice of tomorrow's trouble, and before the day was out he'd paid a visit to the Jarrettville gunsmith and made a second call at the livery stable. My, if them boys coulda seen what was goin' on their eyes woulda jumped clean outta their heads!

The following morning, dead on nine o'clock, Sheriff Morgan checked his Army Colt one more time, pulled on his jacket, pushed his hat firmly on his head and stepped out into the pale sunlight to conduct his regular round of the town in his care. He would play it cool, he decided, observing his usual procedures every step of the way, except that today his right hand would never move far from the weapon holstered at his side. Not that J.J. didn't feel in control; he'd had time to figure out what was likely to happen and he reckoned he had it all worked out. So it didn't surprise him, as he made his rounds, to see them ornery-lookin' strangers cluttering up the boardwalk across from the bank, or to find the Rev. Holliman's wagon standing behind the church with the horses hitched and ready to go. What did alarm him, though, was noticing for the first time how handy the church was for anyone fixin' to give covering fire to a raid on the Jarrettville Bank. 'Have to watch that angle,' he told himself as he headed on down the street, 'or the Reverend's praying could cause me a measure o' pain.'

Down the other end of town young Tom and Chuck were watchin' the Sheriff's every move from the livery stable's hay-loft, determined not to miss any action and tellin' each other what a real hero their Sheriff was. Funny how their opinion of the man had changed since they'd begun to think they might see that fast draw o' his!

Back at his office, J.J. set to loadin' a shotgun and tucked some spare cartridges in his belt, just in case. Then he stepped back on to the street to watch those strangers and to wait for the ranchers' payroll money to come in. It was due at eleven o'clock and that was when J.J. expected them varmints to make their move.

But at 11.03 the pay wagon and its guards came thundering into town, and at 11.14 it thundered out again – and things was still peaceful.

Now, that kinda threw Sheriff Morgan. He'd been watchin' them jackals while the money was bein' unloaded and taken inside the bank, and they'd barely moved enough to scratch an itch.

'Doggone it,' J.J. muttered as he headed back across the street, 'they wasn't after the payroll after all.' Then he stopped and turned to look at 'em again – the man in black, the scruffy one with the scars, the slit-eyed Mexican – and he knew by the way they was starin' back at him that it wasn't over yet. 'So what the heck *are* them fellers after?' he asked himself. Then his eyes went beyond to the church building at the far end of the street, and he set to wonderin'. He was still wonderin' as he turned and headed across to the telegraph office where he wrote out a cable and handed it to the operator. 'That's real urgent, Clyde,' he said. 'I'd be glad if you'd give it priority.'

Well, when the cabled reply came back J. J. Morgan was as pleased as a dog with a bag o' bones. 'So that's their game!' he said with a grin, and headed out the door. He figured he knew how to handle them from now on. What he didn't figure on was young Tom and Chuck gallopin' up and down the street on make-believe horses. 'Hey, boys,' he called, 'I wanna see you in my office.'

'More deputy work?' asked Tom – but J.J. wouldn't say a word till he had them boys behind closed doors.

'Now listen, there's gonna be some shootin' and I want

you fellers off the street.'

'Aw, J.J. – ' moaned Tom, but that was as far as he got
'cause another voice – a rough, mocking voice – broke
in on them from outside.

'Hey, Morgan, let's see how good you are with that
gun – if you ain't too yeller to use it!'

Quick as a flash J.J. pushed the boys to the floor and
went swiftly to the window, sneaking a look down the
street. Just as he'd expected, the street had cleared and
those three jackals stood waitin', hands clawed over their
guns.

'Come on out, you heap o' dirt,' roared Scar-face.

'Try taking our guns *thees* time!' the Mexican snarled.

J.J. allowed himself a slow smile, then glanced at Tom
and Chuck. 'Well, boys,' he said, 'you was wantin' a
showdown.' Then he checked his pistol one more time
and went for the door.

'B-but you can't go out there,' stammered Tom.
'There's *three* of 'em!'

'Ain't you scared?' asked Chuck. 'I mean, them fellers
is *mean*.'

J.J. turned in the doorway and stood lookin' down at
the boy. 'Well, son, at times like this I think on what the
Good Book says: "The fear of man bringeth a snare, but
whoso putteth his trust in the Lord shall be safe." That
seems like good advice to me. Besides' – and he winked
– 'you don't have to be scared when you've taken
precautions!'

J.J. was out the door before the boys could make sense
of that one – and then, like the couple o' monkeys they
were, they sprang to the window and stood peering out
into the street, their eyes wide and their hearts
pounding. 'L-like I said,' muttered Tom, 'them fellers is
mean enough just to *look* someone to death.'

Now J.J. might have been thinking the same thing if
at that moment he hadn't felt that old knee wound

suddenly tighten up, and if memories of that gunfight in Banyon City hadn't flashed through his mind. After that, he was mighty glad to think that those buzzards could do him no harm. 'I oughtta warn you fellers,' he called out, 'that this ain't gonna be a fair fight.'

'You're breaking my heart,' scoffed the silver pistols.

'No,' said Sheriff Morgan, stepping into the street, 'I mean it ain't gonna be fair on *you*. Y'see, the guns you're wearin' – I changed the bullets for blanks.'

Scar-face spat on the ground. 'You can't bluff your way out, Morgan. Now get ready to draw – we wanna see if the famous gunfighter is as fast as they say.'

J.J. shook his head. 'Suit yourselves, but when I found those guns in the Reverend's wagon I was darned if I was gonna leave 'em loaded with live shells. Now you boys can either hand over your irons or start shootin' blanks – the choice is yours.'

Tom and Chuck glanced at each other. *The Reverend's wagon?*

'Eet's a trick,' growled the Mexican. 'Keel him!'

Now, if them boys hadn't seen it for themselves they wouldn't have believed how fast those varmints' guns came outta their holsters.

Better still was the look on their faces when they started throwin' lead – or tried to – and found themselves makin' a whole lot o' noise but not hittin' a thing – especially J. J. Morgan. Fact is, he was just standin' there laughin'. Boy, was they mad!

But best of all was when J.J. decided to wind up the show and went for his gun. Nobody – but nobody – had ever seen a six-gun move so fast. In a blur, that old Army Colt leapt into J.J.'s hand and began spitting flame as one bullet chased another and them fellers' pistols went spinning from their hands. They didn't look quite so menacing then! Truth is, two of 'em gave up right there, but the Mexican was a stubborn character. He

51

went for that long-bladed knife strapped to his boot and let it fly straight at J.J.'s chest. At the same moment, the Sheriff hit the dirt and squeezed off one more round that caught the Mexican in the shoulder and sent him crashing to the ground like a felled pine.

Yessir, the boys got their showdown that day. 'Wow!' was all Tom could say – and Chuck didn't care to disagree with him.

Now all this happened down the street from the church, which was how J.J. had hoped it would be because he didn't want the Rev. Holliman watching the showdown. In fact he wanted the preacher to get a very misleadin' report of what had happened outside the Sheriff's office, and for that reason he sent Tom and Chuck running through the town, shouting out that he'd been shot. 'They got the Sheriff!' Tom cried. 'J.J.'s been hit!' Chuck wailed. And all the time the lawman was playing for time while he locked up them three rattlesnakes and had someone fetch the doc for the Mexican.

'Now don't you worry,' J.J. had told 'em. 'By the time you get round to the church I'll be right behind you.' And he was. He caught up with the boys just a store away and pulled them aside, outta harm's way. 'Wait here while I go in after Holliman,' he told them. 'He's the trickiest of the bunch.'

'How come?' asked Tom.

'Yeah,' said Chuck, 'what's all this about? We figured them fellers were after the payroll money.'

'Nope,' said J.J., 'that was just a decoy, the same as the gunfight. What it's all about is a phoney preacher and stolen gold.'

'Gold?' chorused the boys.

But J.J. was gone, headin' around the back way to the church – and then he was easin' open the back door as quietly as he knew how. Well, he sure didn't want to disturb the Reverend in his praying!

But, y'know, that preacher sure was a messy pray-er. He had half the floorboards in the church pulled up; there were piles of earth here and there where he'd been diggin' beneath the floor; and to one side the preacher was standing in a hole, working in his shirt-sleeves, liftin' bags o' gold-dust up to the floor.

Behind him the Sheriff levelled his gun. 'Seek and ye shall find — eh, Reverend?'

Holliman spun round and grabbed at a shotgun beside the gold, but J.J. leapt forward and kicked it aside. Slowly, a resigned smile spread across the preacher's face. 'Yes, seek and ye shall find — and I found it. You must admit, it was a good try, Sheriff.'

J.J. nodded. 'A real fancy plan, Reverend — although I guess I should stop callin' you that now.'

Holliman climbed out of the hole and dusted off his hands. 'Pity,' he said, 'I was just getting to like the idea. Now tell me, Sheriff, just how did you figure it out?'

J.J. pushed back the brim of his hat with the barrel of his Colt. 'Your friends made the first mistake. When they refused to hand over their guns and you intervened, one of 'em called you "Reverend". But there was no way he could've known you was a preacher — or were supposed to be — unless you'd met before. And somehow I couldn't see them fellers as churchgoers. 'Course, now I see that you were just coolin' 'em down — you didn't want 'em fightin' with me before time.'

'Correct,' said Holliman as he settled in a pew. 'But I can't think that such a little slip gave me away.'

'It didn't,' J.J. told him, 'but it got me sorta curious. I only knew for sure when you overplayed your hand in my office.'

'Oh?'

'Remember you quoted that verse, "Seek and ye shall find," and I remarked that it was found in the Book o'

53

Psalms? Well, I was testin' you then – and you failed. Even a preacher still wet behind the ears would know that verse comes from the gospels, from the mouth of the Good Lord himself.'

Holliman shook his head, smiling. 'Pretty smart, Sheriff. I'd heard you were a religious man, but I didn't figure you for a Bible scholar.'

'Well, that's what gave you away,' J.J. went on, 'and so I decided to take a look in your wagon just to see what you had stashed in there. Imagine me findin' all them guns and this pick an' shovel! Mind you, I didn't catch on to the tools at first; I figured you and your friends were plannin' on taking the payroll money, and that you'd be holed up in here to give 'em cover. But when that didn't happen I had to think again, and then I remembered the pick and shovel, and how interested you seemed in that stolen gold.'

'Don't tell me,' Holliman cut in, 'you checked on Wesley Hogan, the man who'd stolen the gold – '

'And discovered that the feller who was sharin' his cell at the time he died was – surprise, surprise – Silas T. Holliman.'

Holliman laughed. 'Smart work, Sheriff.' Then he said, 'Y'know, I was lucky. Hogan wasn't going to tell me anything about where he'd hidden these bags, but on the morning before he died he finally gave me a clue. "If you want that gold you'd better get down on your knees and pray" – that's all he would say. And that had me guessing for a long time. But when I got out of prison a couple of months back I began to ask around, and quite by chance I discovered that the church here was in the process of being built at the very time the robbery took place.'

'I think I can guess the rest,' said the Sheriff. 'Hogan sneaked into town that night after the robbery lookin' for somewhere to stash the gold. This floor was only half boarded at the time, as I recall, so where better! I guess no one would think of lookin' in a church.'

'Hence his clue,' admitted Holliman. He got to his feet and pulled on his jacket. 'Well, I'll say one thing – praying was never such hard work.'

J.J. smiled, 'Y'know what the Good Book says? "Better to get wisdom than gold." That's Proverbs. You shoulda looked it up.' Then he slid the big Colt into its holster, picked up the shotgun and turned the phoney preacher towards the door. 'Let's go.'

But Holliman wasn't through yet. Fact is, that feller was as slippery as an eel in a barrel o' grease, and he still had one more trick up his sleeve. A derringer, no less – and with a flick of his wrist it slid down his arm and into his hand. Turning suddenly, he fired the single-shot weapon and the bullet rammed into J.J.'s chest, sending him sprawlin' among the pews.

Then there was a gasp and – 'J.J.!'

Holliman swung round to see Tom and Chuck standing there lookin' real shook up. 'Y-you killed 'im!' shrieked Tom.

'Shut up,' Holliman barked, 'and get over here against this wall.' He pointed the derringer at them. 'Or else . . .'

'Shan't!' snapped Chuck, gathering his senses. 'There ain't no bullet in that gun an' you know it. You just fired the only shot.'

'And you killed the Sheriff,' blurted Tom. 'They'll hang you for that.'

Holliman threw the derringer to one side and smiled like a jackal about to have lunch. 'Y'know, you kids are mighty smart – too smart for your own good.' And then he turned and dived for the shotgun J.J. had dropped.

'The shovel!' hissed Tom, and Chuck didn't need no more promptin'. He grabbed that tool, swung it around and let it fly just as Holliman was straightening up. Just as Chuck had hoped, it caught the phoney preacher a hefty blow that knocked him sideways, and when he hit the floor he was out cold.

'Hey, what are you kids doin' here?'

Now that was the Sheriff's voice and the boys nearly jumped outta their skins to hear him sound so alive – and him with a bullet-hole clean through his jacket.

'J.J.! You're all right!' beamed Tom, and he rushed forward to help the Sheriff sit up.

'B-but he shot you – *dead*!' blurted Chuck.

J.J. smiled and pushed a finger through the hole in his coat. 'Well, he shot me, that's for sure . . . but I guess he didn't figure on this!' And with a big grin he pulled out his chunky little Bible . . . with the derringer slug lodged deep inside.

'Hey, how about that!' laughed Chuck.

'Gee,' said Tom, 'that old book stopped the bullet!'

Still smiling, Sheriff Morgan got to his feet. 'There, what did I tell you boys? Make friends with the Bible – you never can tell when it might save your hide!'

Jacob's Run

I caught my first rhino when I was thirteen years of age. If that sounds like an exaggeration I ought to explain that I wasn't exactly alone at the time; in fact I was one of thirty-eight people on the team that year, and the only reason I was there was because the Game Warden in charge just happened to be my father.

Dad had planned the operation under the direction of our National Parks and Wildlife Department in an attempt to save the black rhino from extinction in our part of southern Africa. It was a vital rescue operation to ensure the species survived the relentless hunting and poaching that had claimed many thousands of rhinos even in my own short lifetime.

I was fortunate that the Department had not objected to my going along. Not that the authorities were my biggest problem – that was Dad! He had not wanted me to follow in his footsteps and become a ranger, and so he had sent me to school in England. He said it would give me a broader outlook and the chance to follow my own chosen profession, but all it did was convince me of how much I loved Dad's world. I just lived for the holidays when I could get back home and go out with Dad on his rounds. That was all I ever wanted – to be out in the bush with the animals beneath that big, burning sky. I never thought for a moment of doing any other job. And when I heard about the rhino hunt I was determined to join the team, despite Dad's insistence that it would be too dangerous for me. But I guess Dad knew I wasn't going to take no for an answer – I inherited his stubbornness as well as his love of animals! – and so it was agreed.

That July I just couldn't get home from England quickly enough, for I knew it was going to be an action-packed five weeks, and great experience for a would-be ranger. I would learn a lot, I knew, not only from Dad but from the other rangers, too. I figured that between them they knew everything there was to know about the job, and even if I did nothing more than watch them at work I'd learn plenty. And I did.

Yet, as it turned out, perhaps the most valuable lesson I learned that African winter came not from Dad or his men, but from Jacob, the old African tracker.

I had known Jacob for a long time. In fact he'd been around ever since I could remember, occasionally helping Dad with some job or other, or reporting on the activity of local poachers. But I suppose I'd never taken a great deal of notice of him before. And I certainly wouldn't think so much of him now if I hadn't got to know him on that trip.

He turned up at the ranger station a couple of days before we were due to depart, a tall, gangly figure in tattered shorts and an old string vest. As always, he was barefoot, and on his head, covering much of his greying hair, he wore a rainbow-coloured woollen hat.

During those two days I got talking to Jacob for the first time as we worked with Dad and Ranger Hicks to load the Land-Rovers and pick-up trucks ready for our Friday start, but it wasn't until the convoy was well into the journey that we began talking rhinos. We had left at first light, heading up country to collect the thirty native helpers Dad had engaged, and then swinging west through the foothills towards the place Ranger Hicks had selected for our camp the previous week. This was hundreds of miles from our station in a remote area where the rhinos were particularly vulnerable to poachers. As Dad said, this was the only place to start. I said as much to Jacob as we bounced along in the back of our pick-up, perched on top of the meal-sacks.

The old African nodded. 'You know much about the rhinoceros?'

'Only what I've read and what Dad's told me,' I replied.

The truck shook as we hit a rut. 'The rhino, he is a magnificent creature – but he is a mean one.'

'I know,' I said, 'but not as mean as the poachers. When I was home last time, Dad took me out to see a rhino carcass, the remains of a bull that had been snared by poachers. There was a steel cable around one of its hind legs and a noose around its neck. Dad said it probably took three days to die. All for its horn and hide. It's the poachers who are mean.'

'This is true,' said Jacob. 'If you must track one or the other, track rhino. If the poachers catch you they will shoot you, spear you, or cut off your head. And they will enjoy it. Rhino will do only what he has to and as quickly as he can.' He paused, looking out across the vast African wastelands, mile after mile of dry, hard earth. 'Yes, rhino is mean,' he said, 'but he is not cruel. Only man is cruel.'

He seemed to be distant, as though remembering something, and I asked him if he'd ever come face to face with the poachers.

Jacob laughed, baring the few teeth left in his old head. Then he held up three long, black fingers. 'Three times they try to kill me because I help the rangers. Three times I run.' He laughed again, slapping his bony knee. 'Long legs, see? No one could catch old Jacob.'

I nodded, picturing in my mind those vicious men chasing this likeable old man, though of course he may have been a lot younger then. 'Were you afraid?' I asked.

He thought about it. 'Yes, but that fear did not last long. Jacob was more afraid for the animals – afraid of what the poachers would do to them.'

I sat secretly admiring him. 'You love animals, don't you?'

He nodded, smiling. 'I love all God's creatures.'

About a mile down river we turned off and cut across country again, weaving our way among the boabab trees and heading through Chief Magosa's territory towards our destination in the distant hills. Jacob told me that at one time the whole area had teemed with wildlife – lion, wart-hog, all kinds of buck, zebra, rhino – but persistent trapping by Magosa's people, plus years of plundering by the professional poachers, had whittled down the numbers until now few remained. Yet the senseless killing continued.

When I heard this I felt even more determined to see our rescue operation get under way, and as the convoy at last pulled into the clearing which Ranger Hicks had chosen for us I couldn't wait for the tracking to begin. First, though, we had to set up camp – a substantial base from which we could strike out each day – and after Ranger Hicks had marked out positions for everything we set to work. Over there in the waist-high yellow grass we were to erect the sleeping tents. On the edge of the clearing would be the catering area with the supplies stacked beneath tarpaulins, and behind these, along with the all-important water tank, were the almost equally vital fuel-drums. On the far side of the clearing, to the north, we would set up our 'operational HQ', a wide tent with a portable table where each morning the rangers would plan the day's programme, and each evening log the progress made. Behind that, built of stout logs roped together and standing ten feet high, would be the stockade for the rhinos. In the centre of the clearing would be a huge camp fire which was to be kept burning throughout our stay. This, as much as anything, was to be essential to our comfort during the hours spent in camp, for the July nights were as cold as the days were hot.

Working together under the rangers' instructions we had the whole camp established by evening, and after my first night's sleep out in the bush I was ready for our first rhino. But over breakfast of meal-cakes and coffee I discovered that the hunt had begun long before I had crawled from my tent. Jacob and his game scouts had left camp while it was still dark and had been out on foot searching for any sign of fresh spoor. Yesterday's tracks, I learned, were no use. Rhinos move around a great deal and in order to track and catch one in a day you need to start not too many miles behind it. Only today's spoor will lead you to it, and then only if you move fast. But to begin with it's all down to the tracker and his scouts. This morning they had done well.

The news came through on the two-way radio: fresh spoor south of the Ganga river. The hunt was on! We grabbed our things, ran for the trucks and threw ourselves aboard, latecomers hurling themselves at the tail-boards through the choking dust as tyres spun and the convoy moved out. No soft ride on the meal-sacks this time. Every jolt and jar of that shuddering journey went hammering through our bodies, and it seemed as if it would go on for ever as we sped across that wild country, up hills, down into ravines, and back up on to the dust-plains. And all the while the fierce white sun beat mercilessly down.

But then, at last, someone was shouting, 'Ganga! Ganga!' and we were nearly there. Down the shifting bank, along by the dry river-bed and up into the gentle hill-country beyond.

'Good work,' said Dad when Jacob showed him the first spoor just beyond a humpy ridge. We gathered round as Jacob squatted to show us his find and I knelt beside him. There wasn't much to see, just a small moon-shaped mark on the ground with a little wrinkled pattern beside it — the toe and pad of a rhinoceros.

'Does it look good ahead?' Dad asked. He knew that Jacob and the scouts would already have tried to follow the trail.

The old man nodded. 'But we could use some help.' And as he said it he held out his hand and looked up at the cloudless sky.

Dad laughed. 'Look, if it rains I'll be able to find the blighter myself and you'll be out of a job.'

With that Jacob roared with laughter, adjusted his colourful hat and went padding off with the game scouts at his heels.

Dad glanced down at me, grinning. 'He's got a nerve,' he said. 'He wants it to rain so that the ground will soften up and he can see the spoor more easily. He knows full well it won't rain for weeks yet.'

I turned to examine the spoor again. 'I suppose we just have to be thankful for the dust, then.'

Dad came and knelt beside me and ran his fingers through Jacob's find, breaking up the pattern. 'You're right there, son. This ground is so hard, without the dust there'd be no trail at all.'

Back at the vehicles Ranger Hicks organized the helpers who were to carry the guns, water-flasks, radio and other essential equipment, and we set off, leaving two of the other rangers and the rest of the African helpers to wait for our call when we had bagged our rhino. When that call came they would have to drive like fury to get the big pick-up in to us, and together we would work fast to load the animal aboard.

For the first hour we moved quickly across that wild country, keeping close behind Jacob and the scouts as they led us first to one and then another of the spoor they had discovered since they had first alerted us by radio. Then, as the hunt began for fresh signs of our rhino's trail, we slackened the pace and strung out while the old African went ahead. Each time he found more spoor he would turn and wave at us, never shouting lest the rhino should hear him and take flight.

'Their hearing is very acute,' Dad reminded me as we trudged on beneath the boiling sun. 'Their eyesight's poor, of course, but if you get upwind of them they'll hear you from miles away. And once they're startled they'll either take off and lose you or turn and charge.'

'So we have to take him by surprise,' I said. 'Creep up on him without him suspecting a thing.'

Dad nodded. 'That's the way we like to do it, son.'

But we weren't to do any creeping for hours yet. That rhino's path took us across mile after mile of open country, through ravines, up into the hills and back down on to the plain. The going was tough all the way – it was hot, dusty, tiring work – and by the time Jacob said we were close we must have walked more than fifteen miles. What I would have given for a cool swim or refreshing shower! And yet, when at last we set eyes on our rhino, all discomfort simply melted away. There he was: the black rhinoceros!

We saw him first in the late afternoon light, about a hundred metres away on top of a small rise. He was magnificent. A great, proud beast, easily the height of a man, a good 2000lb of lumbering power, and with that deadly horn jutting into the western sky. A beast that could kill a man with a mere flick of its head, a beast notorious for its quick temper.

I glanced anxiously at Jacob crouched beside me. Dad had already signalled us not to talk, but Jacob did a little mime for me, explaining that if the rhino charged we would have to scramble up into the trees behind us. That was the only safe place. I nodded, thanking him, and when I looked again Dad was moving forward to the cover of some boulders, the tranquillizer gun crooked in his arm. At the same time Ranger Hicks was taking up a covering position, levelling the rhino in his sights in case things went badly wrong.

But it looked as if everything was going to be all right. The rhino was not yet aware of us and Dad was closing on him. Another ten metres and he would be in range.

Then, in a split second, everything changed. The great horned head swung up, the rhino's ears twitched wildly, and he brought his massive bulk around to face us. The wind had shifted and the beast had got our scent.

Ahead of us, Dad froze to the spot, not daring to move and willing the rhino to turn away, to settle down again. But the rhino was disturbed now, sensing danger. Slowly, he started towards us, his great horn slicing the air as his head tossed first this way and then that.

Ahead I heard Dad curse as he brought up the tranquillizer gun, slammed the dart into the breech and raised the butt to his shoulder. Then he was stepping out from his cover, lining up his target in the sights and muttering to himself. 'All right, feller,' I heard him say. 'Let's be having you.'

As though responding, the rhino picked up speed, its head down for the charge and the thunderous pounding of its feet sending tremors shuddering through the ground beneath us.

In that instant I was plunged into nightmare. This enormous, snorting beast was coming straight for us. The sabre-like horn was lowered for attack. Two thousand pounds of violent death were closing for the kill. There was no escape now. No point even in running. Trembling, I watched the end of our lives hurtle towards us. Seventy metres, sixty, fifty . . .

Crack! The silver dart flashed from the rifle and flew to the rhino's forehead. Then another, smaller explosion as the dart discharged its drug . . . a whirl of the massive head . . . a bellowing grunt . . . and a cry from Jacob!

'The trees! Make for the trees!'

With legs of lead I stumbled for the nearest branches and was pulled to safety only seconds before the great horn hammered into the solid trunk. The whole tree shook and I locked my arms round a branch.

A second crash, a third, and then the huge dust-sprayed hide was passing beneath us, the beast suddenly having lost all interest in his enemy. Still shaking, we watched it lumbering off over the ridge and out of sight.

I breathed again – but then panic struck once more as I swung round on my branch. 'Where's Dad?'

My tree companion pointed. With a huge smile on his tanned face, Dad was climbing out from the cover of some rocks, holding the dart gun high over his head in triumph.

I slid from the tree as Dad approached. 'How long before the drug works?'

He wiped the perspiration from his face with his sleeve. 'Give it twenty minutes and he'll be flat out.' He looked around as Jacob and the scouts took off on the rhino's trail. 'Come on, son,' he said, 'we have to track him down before the light goes. If we lose him now we'll have to start all over again in the morning.'

I nodded and fell into step with Dad as he took off. I already knew that the tranquillizer wouldn't last much longer than four or five hours. 'We won't lose him,' I said, 'not with Jacob up front.'

Half an hour later, and about three miles away, we found the rhino collapsed to the ground in a hollow. The Africans were already there, fussing around the slumbering giant and laughing like little kids. All their lives they had been told it was impossible to catch a rhino alive. They just couldn't believe it!

Dad walked slowly around the rhinoceros, smiling with satisfaction and occasionally slapping the beast's black hide. Then he turned to Ranger Hicks. 'Get

Dawson on the radio and tell him to move that truck.'

We didn't get to bed very early that night. Getting the rhino into the truck was a two-hour job that involved thirty men pushing, heaving, winching and rolling our catch on to a wooden sled and then up specially made steel runners. Then, with the rhino firmly lashed down, there was the long, jolting drive through the darkness, and then all the work of getting the beast into the stockade back at camp. There Dad rammed a syringe of tranquillizer into its rump, gave it a shot of a booster drug, and posted a couple of African workers to watch from the top of the stockade, just to make sure that our rhino recovered without complications. Finally, late into the night, we went off to sink down by the blazing camp fire with a bowl of steaming broth and a fistful of bread.

I don't think I've ever felt as tired as I did that night, but we were all far too excited to sleep and so we sat around the fire, reliving the hunt and savouring our success. At least one black rhino would be kept from the poachers' snares. That felt good! And somehow we knew that this animal would be the first of many.

'So you have caught a rhinoceros!'

I turned to see Jacob grinning down at me, an enamel mug in his bony hand. 'I didn't do much,' I said. 'Besides, you *found* the rhino. In a sense *you* caught him.'

The old African laughed and squatted down beside me, adjusting his woollen hat. 'To find him is one thing. To make him sleep and carry him away in a truck is another.'

I nodded. 'But I still think you're clever, Jacob, chasing across country and finding those spoor marks.'

He shook his head. 'Rhino – he is the clever one. Jacob needs to see spoor to track rhino, but rhino will track Jacob just by smelling him. Rhino bright, Jacob dim.'

66

'Not at all,' I said. 'I wish *I* could track animals the way you do.'

He sat looking into the fire. 'It is not difficult, if you will take time to observe what has been created. That way you get to know the way things are — why a buck feeds here and not there, why the lion hunts at this time and not that, why the rhino uses this hill, but not that one . . .'

'Is that the secret?'

He nodded. 'Keep your eyes open, desire to understand, and in time you will begin to think like the animal you are tracking.'

'And that's all there is to it?'

Jacob considered this for a moment. 'Almost.' He turned to me with mischief in his eyes. 'Sometimes,' he went on, 'I cheat.'

'You *cheat?*'

He laughed aloud. 'If Jacob cannot find the trail he asks Jesus which way.'

I stared at him. 'You ask *Jesus?*'

He shrugged his shoulders. 'Why not? He made the world and everything in it, so Jacob figures he ought to know which way his rhino went. He does, too. He has not been wrong yet, when Jacob hears him right.' He looked at me. 'You see? Jacob is not so clever after all. I had to ask him today.'

I sat gazing into the warming blaze of our fire, wondering what to make of the old African. Did he really believe that Jesus talked to him? Or that God even cared about helping him track animals?

He shifted beside me. 'Your father says that you want to be a Game Warden, just like him. Is this so?'

I glanced at Jacob, nodding. 'He didn't want me to get involved unless I really wanted nothing else. That's why he sent me to school in England, so that I'd feel free to choose my own career. I think he hoped I'd get interested in banking or law or something like that, but all England did for me was to make me long to be back here, out in the bush.'

Jacob smiled. 'You have a heart after God,' he said. 'You care about his world. Your father has realized this is so, or you would not be here.'

I turned to face him. 'I'm not so sure Dad thinks I'm cut out for this sort of work, Jacob. You remember I told you about Dad taking me to see the remains of a rhino that had been snared by poachers? Well, I think he did that to try to put me off. But I *wasn't* put off. It was horrible, yes, but it simply made me more determined than ever that I would spend my life trying to help the animals. The trouble was, when I saw that butchered rhino I – I cried. It sounds so foolish now. Dad was really angry about that rhino – but I just cried.'

He smiled at me. 'Tears are good. Jacob has known your father many years and remembers when he too cried for a snared animal.'

I stared at him. 'Is that right?'

'Perhaps he has forgotten, but Jacob does not forget.' He paused, then said again. 'Tears are good. Only he with a heart of stone never cries, and a heart of stone will not make a good ranger.'

I smiled. 'Thank you, Jacob. I *hope* I make a good ranger – I certainly want to try.'

'You will,' he said, 'but you will be a better one still if you learn to look at the world through the eyes of God and to listen with his ears.'

I wondered whether to ignore this, but curiosity got the better of me. 'How do I do that?'

The old African grinned and drained his mug. 'God hears the grass growing, and sees the wind before it stirs the leaves, and knows where every drop of rain will fall before it leaves the sky. If you open your heart to him and seek to love his world as much as he does, perhaps you too will hear and see and know.'

I stared at him, wide-eyed. 'Do *you* hear these things? *See* the wind?'

He shook his head and shuffled a little closer to the fire. 'No. But perhaps one day. The way I see it, the closer Jacob gets to God, the more he will be like him.'

In the first week we captured five rhinos, and when the pens in the stockade were full we brought in some big trucks, got the beasts into reinforced crates, hoisted them aboard and sent them off to the safety of the game reserve. There, at last, they would be free from the threat of the poachers; free to live out their lives in peace.

While those rhinos were on their way we continued the rescue operation, eventually increasing our rate of success until, by the third week, we were bringing in one rhino almost every night. Many of these had snare scars, a fact that spurred us on and made us even more determined to get the rhinos out of the poachers' reach — but it also meant that the pace became gruelling. This was particularly true for Jacob and the scouts whose long day started so much earlier than our own, and as time went by I could see that the old African was beginning to tire.

The heat didn't help. It was now late August and with the long African winter drawing to a close the days were getting hotter. The Africans were used to the temperatures, of course, and most seemed unaffected; but I noticed that Jacob was stopping for more and more rests. One day I saw him squatting after tracking spoor. He seemed very weary and looked very old. The accident happened the next day.

It was late afternoon and our party was strung out about two hundred metres behind Jacob and the scouts. The trail had taken them through dry river-bed, up into the hills, down to the plain, and finally to an area where there was much *jesse* – thick, tangled undergrowth. The African scouts were about fifty metres from this, apparently discussing whether to go into the bush in search of our rhino, when their minds were made up for them.

It came thundering at them – the biggest bull rhino we had seen on the whole trip. Head down, the murderous horn set to kill, it catapulted from the undergrowth, bellowing its rage. Shrieks of terror went up from the scouts as they scattered and ran for their lives. Even old Jacob sprinted away with astonishing speed – but his line of escape was directly ahead of the maddened bull and it was he whom the rhino picked out as the target for its wrath.

For long moments we watched, transfixed with horror, and then Dad started yelling for the bearers to bring the guns. Seconds later he and Ranger Hicks were pounding across the open ground, loading the rifles as they ran, and yelling at the tops of their voices to try to distract the rhino.

It was no use. The bull had it in for Jacob. It was gaining on him, too, and there was no cover ahead – not so much as a solitary tree. With a glance over his shoulder, Jacob began zig-zagging, those long legs twisting and turning, but the rhino stayed with him, storming closer by the second.

It was a living nightmare. From the top of our rise we watched helplessly while the life-or-death chase dragged on. First Jacob went this way, then that, but always that deadly horn was behind him.

'Turn, Jacob, turn!' I yelled. 'Head for the *jesse*!'

I think he heard me because almost immediately he started to swing round in a curve and began striding back towards the undergrowth, now about two hundred metres away. But the rhino was swift and pounded after him, those enormous feet now moving even faster as they kicked great clouds of dust into the air.

It was then, on the beast's turn, that Dad fell to one knee and let off three rounds. Ranger Hicks fired more shots, but only two bullets found their mark, striking the rhino's flank. These slowed the bull for only a moment, and then it seemed to throw itself forward even faster, probably incensed by the burning pain in its side.

'Faster, Jacob!' I heard Dad shout as he brought the rifle to his shoulder again. 'Run, man, run!'

Another glance over his shoulder and Jacob must have sensed that time was running out. Those powerful legs that had kept him from death at the hands of the poachers, and probably had saved him from the jaws of many a wild animal, were now beginning to tire and he must have known that he'd never beat the rhino to the *jesse*. That was when he turned and began running straight towards the rifles, hoping that Dad or Ranger Hicks could stop the beast with a bullet in its head.

But with Jacob in the way the men couldn't get a clear shot at the bull and hesitated. That was when it happened.

The rhino closed . . . the horn rammed home . . . the old African screamed . . . the fierce head whirled . . . and the limp body flew through the air and crashed to earth.

As the beast swung round to attack again the rifles barked – once, twice, three times – and the massive rhino, its huge horn glistening with blood, crashed to the ground, snorting its rage. Two more bullets at close range and it was dead.

When I reached Jacob he was sweating and shivering at the same time, and blood was soaking through the bush-jacket Ranger Hicks had thrown over him.

'We'll get you to hospital, Jacob,' I blurted.

The old face cracked in a weary smile. 'Jacob don't need no hospital,' he said. 'That old bull made a good job of it.'

I looked at Dad — surely there was something we could do — but he shook his head.

Jacob coughed and blood trickled from his mouth. 'I'm sure sorry about the rhino, warden. That was a fine animal. It should have lived.'

Dad nodded. 'So should you, Jacob. And you're more important. We'll catch another rhino, but there's no one going to take *your* place.'

The African smiled weakly, but then pain shot through him and he screwed up his face. When the spasm had passed he said, 'We did well, though. Many rhinos will now be safe.'

'Many,' said Dad. 'And it's largely thanks to you, Jacob. You're the best tracker I ever had.'

Jacob looked pleased and lay savouring the compliment. Then he said, 'Warden, this boy o' yours wants to be a ranger like you — you know that?'

Dad glanced at me. 'I know it, Jacob.'

'Well, you let him be just that, huh? He's a fine boy — make a good ranger.' He winced with pain. 'You hear me, warden?'

Dad rolled up his bush-jacket and eased it under Jacob's head. 'I hear you, old man. And don't you worry — he'll make a fine warden.'

Dad glanced at me again, smiling faintly, but at that moment my own future didn't seem to matter. I looked down at Jacob, my throat tight and my eyes full. 'Isn't there anything we can do for you, Jacob? Anything you want?'

He smiled weakly. 'I don't need nothin' now, son. Why, I got everything I need.' He turned his eyes to the sky. 'Just listen to that!'

I strained my ears but heard nothing except the distant call of a guinea-fowl. Somehow I knew he didn't mean that. 'What is it, Jacob?'

His eyes closed and he smiled again. 'The sweetest

sound,' he said. 'I knew I'd hear it one day.'

I understood now. 'You hear the grass growing? Is that it? What's it like?'

'Music,' he said. 'Sweet music.'

And then he died.

We captured thirty-seven rhinos on that first trip, and the following year we rounded up another twenty-nine, so that by my fifteenth birthday there were sixty-six black rhinos scattered through the 1,800 square miles of the Kirimunda Game Reserve. Under that special protection many calves have been born over the years, and today the rhinos number more than one hundred. We hope that in the years to come there will be many more, and perhaps in a few generations from now there may even be sufficient to justify removing *Diceros bicornis*, the black rhinoceros, from today's long list of endangered species.

Out here in the bush, however, it's a very different story, for the rhino has more or less been hunted out of existence. There are a few left, though — in fact only the other day I saw the rare sight of a rhino cow with her young calf down at the watering hole near Jacob's Run.

It's funny how that tag has stuck all these years. I think it was one of the scouts who first called that stretch of rugged country west of the river by that name, and though you won't find the words on any map you could ask anyone within a thousand miles of this place and they would tell you all about it.

To me, of course, Jacob's Run is a special place and always will be. I get out there from time to time because it's part of my territory, just as it used to be part of Dad's, and occasionally, when I need to think things through, I'll drive out there just to remember, and to soak in the peculiar peace that the place has for me. Perhaps that's surprising, considering the violent death that occurred there all those years ago, but I never think about that. Instead I recall that old African – that very special man – who taught me many things, including one of the most valuable lessons I have ever learned – a lesson that even someone who spends all his time out here in the wilds might easily have missed.

This world, with all the beauty, mystery and terror of living things, is *God's* world. I see it best when I see it through his eyes.

Earl's
First Christmas

'Merry Christmas, Earl.'

On 25 December, 2098, Colonel Earl T. Parker of the United States Space Force awoke to hear this greeting being bleeped at him by the electronic voice of his personal computer. Slowly, very slowly, the astronaut opened his eyes and for several seconds lay watching the floating sphere that had been his constant companion for almost five months. Slightly larger than a soccer ball and about the same weight, the sphere hung in the pressurized sleep-chamber like a giant Christmas tree decoration – a huge glass 'bauble', its deep purple sheen gently reflecting the soft overhead lighting. But it would have been a very rich man indeed who could have afforded to hang *this* bauble on his tree. Deep beneath its surface a bank of lights glimmered in response to the human eye-contact and a million electronic thoughts raced through its complex memory bank in search of the correct reaction to a human who had been wished 'Merry Christmas' but failed to respond. But wait, the lips were moving . . .

'Humbug!' said the astronaut at last, and closed his eyes again.

The computer bleeped its surprise and searched again for the appropriate response. Humbug? What did 'humbug' have to do with Christmas? It found the answer deep within its micro-chip library under the heading 'Literary Classics'. Within a millionth of a second it had scanned the entire works of Charles Dickens, found *A Christmas Carol*, and fed the relevant information through the section of the brain that controlled voice facility.

'Oh, come on now, Colonel, do you really feel as grouchy about Christmas as old Scrooge?'

The eyes opened again and the lips moved in a faint smile. 'Almost. Now move over, Arthur, and let me get up.'

Instantly the computer hovered sideways and Earl swung his legs off the bed and sat up on its edge. As he did so Arthur emitted a low hum that Earl always interpreted as a 'sympathy buzz'. It was one of the lifelike capacities that Arthur's designer had built into his electronic personality – a feature that normally was appreciated. But right now it irritated Earl into thinking about taking his personal computer down to the leisure section for a game of ten-pin bowling.

He pulled on his worksuit and stood up, looking Arthur in his eye-sensor. 'Do you realize this is the first time in my entire life that I have had to spend Christmas alone?'

Arthur said nothing as the events of the past twenty-four hours filtered through his 'memory recall': the groanings of Earl's partner, Brad Crawford, as he lay writhing with pain . . . Earl's vain attempts to administer relief through anything to be found in the medical bay . . . the inevitable call to Ground Control for help . . . the arrival of the astro-medics and their decision to take Brad off the space-station and operate on the return journey to earth . . . Earl's request for an immediate replacement and Control's promise to send one.

'Well, you guys make sure you find one,' Earl had told them. 'It was bad enough the *two* of us being stuck up here for Christmas, thirty thousand miles from home, but if I have to spend Christmas Day alone I'll go bananas.'

'Sure, sure,' the Controller had said soothingly, 'but

it's not going to be easy finding a replacement on Christmas Eve. I'll do my best, Colonel, that's all I can promise.'

But Earl's hourly check on the situation had failed to offer any glimmer of hope and by the time he turned in he had resigned himself to spending Christmas alone with the computers.

Arthur thought about it for a moment and gave another sympathy buzz.

'Cut it out, will you,' the astronaut snapped as he ran the laser-shaver over his chin. 'Talk to me if you must, Arthur, but forget the condolences.'

'Sorry,' bleeped Arthur – and from that the Colonel knew his electronic companion was trying extra hard. A computer of his ability never got things wrong and therefore never needed to apologize. He was really stretching his circuits to provide such a conciliatory response as 'Sorry'.

'Aw, forget it,' Earl smiled. 'I'm just sore about being left to hold the fort while the rest of the human race enjoys itself.'

Arthur gave a series of quick-fire clicks – a confession of confusion. 'I'll never understand you humans, Earl. According to my information most Americans will spend today gorging themselves with unhealthily large amounts of food, and a good proportion will add to the damage by consuming so much alcohol that their mobility will be seriously – if only temporarily – impaired. And you call that enjoying yourself.'

Earl gave a short laugh. 'Yeah, I must admit that does sound kinda crazy. But if we overeat or have a few drinks too many it's just because we're . . . well, happy.'

Arthur clicked again. 'But if you are happy to begin with, why eat until your stomach protests and drink until your head throbs? Unless such discomfort makes you happier still.'

77

Earl shook his head. 'You don't understand. Christmas is a time for being together with the people you love. In those circumstances people celebrate, and food and drink are part of the – ' He cut himself short, annoyed at having to explain and angered by his predicament. 'Look, just fetch me some coffee. I'll be in the observatory.'

'No breakfast this morning?' There was a hint of reproach in the voice.

'Arthur!' scolded the astronaut. 'You are my personal computer, not my mother. If I don't want my Wheatie-Cubes this morning that is fine with me and it is fine with you. Now get the coffee!'

The rest of the morning went slowly as Earl made heavy work of logging the data monitored by the radio telescopes – the only real job while the programme remained shut down for the holiday – and Arthur hovered in corners emitting self-conscious 'blip-blip' noises. Once or twice he lapsed into humming the tune of a Christmas carol in an attempt to lift his master's spirits, but after Earl had thrown a notebook at him he gave up.

Not even the synthetic roast turkey dinner, complete with trimmings, a cracker and a paper hat, managed to lift the gloom that had settled over the lone astronaut, though Arthur did detect a spark of festive anticipation when Earl brought out a handful of brightly-wrapped Christmas presents, sent up by the regular mail-ship.

But the anticipation, it seemed, was scarcely rewarded. Evidently Earl found little to inspire him in the odd assortment of gifts. Hand-knitted cosmic socks from Auntie Jean; a bottle of 'Starburst' aftershave from Bob and Lucy; low-gravity slippers from Mom and Dad (not slippers again!); and a three-dimensional wallchart of earth's solar system from Arnold, his nephew.

'Space!' he grunted as he sat looking dejectedly at the

confusion of paper and presents in front of him. 'They all thought of me and thought of space. What's the matter? Don't they think I belong on earth? Don't they think I'm ever coming back?'

The mood passed, however, as the time approached for the live link-up with home via the space-phone, and by three in the afternoon (Kentucky time) he was whistling 'Jingle-bells' while he counted down the last minute before dialling the code and switching on the viewer to see his folks waving and grinning at him from the little timber-frame house he knew so well back in his hometown of Anchorage.

His mother was first to lift the personal receiver and wish him 'Merry Christmas', and after she had told him her news and been assured that the slippers would fit, she handed the receiver to Dad. Dad wanted Earl to know how proud he was that his own son was doing such a great job 'pushing back the frontiers of space exploration' and how well their local football team was doing since they'd signed Ed MacDonnell, the big kicker from New York. Then it was Auntie Jean's turn and she told Earl he'd never believe the trouble she had getting the pattern for the cosmic socks, but Earl glanced sideways at the socks and said he would. Next came brother Bob, his wife Lucy, and finally young Arnold. Arnold, it seemed, had the most to say — or rather, the most questions to ask. After thanking his uncle for the terrific video-watch, he wanted to know all about what Earl was doing up there. Was it true what his Dad had told him, that Uncle Earl was now working on some sort of time-travel project?

'Well, that makes it sound a little like science-fiction,' Earl replied. 'What we're doing here is experimenting with possible ways of speeding up the process known as time so as to make deep-space travel a real possibility. I guess you know that time is now the only major barrier preventing us from reaching the planets in our solar system, Arnold. Once we've learned to control it, just about any destination will be within our reach.'

'A day-trip to Mars?' laughed the young face on the screen.

'Why not?' said Earl. 'Mars would be a short hop – like a boat-ride round Liberty Island – once we've learned how to harness the time-factor and make it work for us.'

'Gee!' said the boy, his eyes full of wonder.

Earl laughed. 'Hey, don't get the wrong idea – your uncle isn't some kind of Buck Rogers. This can be as boring as any other job, watching computers, making calculations, programming new data. Most of the real work – the experiments – isn't done by us at all. Big Boy is the brains.'

'Big Boy?'

'Yeah, that's the main computer system. It controls the entire programme with just the occasional nudge from me or my partner.'

'Wow,' said Arnold. 'I sure wish I could see it.'

'Tell you what,' Earl grinned. 'I'll trade places with you. Right now I'd give just about anything to be there with you folks. I'm all alone up here since my partner took sick and it's no fun, no fun at all.'

'All alone?' It was Earl's mother again. She'd been hovering in the wings, waiting to say a quick good-bye before NASA shut down the line, and had taken the receiver from her grandson's hands. 'Why, Earl, that's terrible. Are they sending a replacement?'

'Oh, hi, Mom. Yeah, they tell me they're on top of it, but it doesn't seem likely they'll get anyone up here today.'

'Well, that's just too bad, son. I don't know why they picked you for Christmas duty anyway.'

'Of course you do, Mom. The single guys always get

Christmas duty. If I had a wife and kids I'd be there with you all right now.'

A high-pitched bleep broke in on the conversation, signalling time up.

'Now you be sure to have a great Christmas,' Earl called above the tone.

Earl's Dad nosed into the picture for the final farewell. 'Enjoy yourself as best you can, son. You can get all the TV stations, can't you? They're running some John Wayne on the old Movie Classics channel. We know how you love the Westerns. Bye now, and – '

Silence hit the relaxation bay and Earl slumped back in his chair. In that stark moment the sense of separation was punishing. He breathed deeply and exhaled noisily simply to hear some sound.

'May I make a suggestion, Colonel?'

He swung round in alarm for his thoughts had been far away. 'Arthur! How many times have I told you not to come creeping up on me like that?'

'I did not creep,' the computer protested. 'I *cannot* creep.'

'Don't play word games with me,' the astronaut snapped back.

'Precisely what I was about to suggest,' Arthur informed him. 'I thought, as there was little else to do, you might enjoy one of those three-dimensional crosswords. I've been working on a new grid.'

'Hmmm. I wondered what had been keeping you so quiet. Any other suggestions?'

Arthur bleeped in the affirmative. 'I was going to suggest the John Wayne movies before your father raised the subject. Or . . .'

'Or what?'

Arthur began to hum a deep, vibrating hum which Earl instantly recognized as the computer's signal for mischief. The astronaut eyed him suspiciously. 'Or *what*, Arthur? Let's have it.'

'Well, it occurred to me . . . that is, I wondered if . . . I mean, could I interest you in . . . ?'

'Stop stalling,' Earl warned him. 'What's on your wicked little mind, Arthur?'

'Time-travel,' the computer replied.

'Huh?'

'Your nephew put the idea into my circuits and – well, as it's Christmas I thought some sort of treat was due.' Arthur made a noise like an electronic clearing of the throat. 'What I mean is – '

'*Personal* time-travel?' asked Earl. 'Like, you and me going places?'

'Something like that,' Arthur confessed.

Earl let the idea run free in his mind. 'We could get in a lot o' trouble, pal. I could lose my commission. You could end up on some assembly line counting machine parts.'

'But we'd sure have something to brag about!' Arthur sniggered.

The astronaut grinned and leaned back in his chair. Maybe it wasn't going to be such a dull day after all. 'OK, little buddy, let's hear it.'

Arthur bleeped excitedly. 'Just pick your time and place, Earl. You name it, past, present or future, and with Big Boy's help we can pay a visit. What would you like to see? Some great historic moment? Let's see now – how about the arrival of the *Mayflower* with the Pilgrim Fathers? Or Wyatt Earp's gunfight at the OK Corral? The Wright Brothers' first manned flight? The first moon landing? Or how about selected moments from World War Three?'

'On Christmas Day?' exploded Earl.

'Well, perhaps not,' Arthur conceded. 'But what do you think of the general concept?'

Earl smiled his biggest smile that day. But then his

eyes clouded. 'Big Boy won't allow it. You know how mean he can get − he'll flatly refuse to co-operate.'

'Not if you remove his C1,' Arthur sniggered.

'What?' stormed Earl. 'Unplug his conscience?' Then his frown disappeared and an impish light appeared in his eyes. 'Yeah! Let's do it!'

He set to the task with a boyish glee, an echo of the nine-year-old Earl who had tied his uncle's shoelaces together beneath the kitchen table . . . the boy who had put a frog in his brother's bed at Hallowe'en. This latest prank gave him almost as much pleasure, though it was done in seconds.

'There,' he said, turning to Arthur with a mischievous smile. 'Now all we have to do is programme the time and place.'

But choosing was more difficult than he had expected, and after long moments of indecision he elected to leave the choice to Big Boy. 'Just give us something festive, something seasonal,' he instructed. And with that he retreated to the G-force chamber where he was to remain while the central axis of the station revolved at phenomenal speed − the key to crossing the time-barrier.

He emerged minutes later, swaying a little as he headed for the Control Centre and the awesome wall of electronics that was Big Boy. Instantly his eyes went to the computer's chronometer. 'Hey, look at this!' he exclaimed as Arthur appeared at his shoulder. 'We've run right off the clock, back to nought! What does it mean?' He turned to the floating sphere. 'Is this some kind of joke, Arthur? Has Big Boy spun us back to the dawn of time?'

'Not at all,' came the electronic reply. 'We've merely been transported back to the point in time that marked the beginning of the Christian calendar.'

Earl stared at his computer for a moment, allowing

this to sink in. Then he turned and jabbed a finger at the controls marked 'viewscreens'. In response a bank of monitors blinked into life giving all-round visual contact with the space-world outside. It was just as it had been in his own time. Below, Earth filled the screens, its features unchanged though more clearly defined – an earth whose atmosphere had not yet been choked by pollution. And above, as always, the great panorama of space that he had loved from boyhood. It was a sight that never failed to stir him, and now, as he gazed out into the heavens of more than two thousand years before his time, he found himself marvelling afresh at the beauty and design of it all. But then, in a moment, his sense of wonder turned to intrigue. There was a light out there that he could not identify. A star, perhaps? No, this light was moving swiftly through space. A comet, then? But no comet had ever burned through the darkness at the speed of *this* light. What *could* it be?

Arthur bleeped a chuckle as though Big Boy had played a joke and let him in on it. Earl glanced at him uncertainly, then ran his fingers over the controls that brought the giant telescopes into play. Immediately the tracking equipment found its mark and steadily beamed in on the mysterious light. Within three seconds Earl knew what it was, though his mind couldn't take it in.

'*Angels?*'

As the radio signals bounced back even closer pictures Earl's eyes began to widen. 'Arthur, am I seeing straight? Do I see angels?'

'Well, you did ask for something seasonal,' the computer replied.

For long seconds Earl stood watching the screen in stunned silence, wondering whether he was dreaming and wishing someone was there to pinch him. In his studies of the heavens he had made many exciting discoveries and encountered strange and wonderful phenomena, but this beat the lot. Hosts of angels – how many were there? hundreds? thousands? – zooming through space as though on some divine mission!

Divine mission! Suddenly his mind was racing and he turned to Arthur with a great excitement in his eyes. 'What did you say, Arthur?'

The computer gave a startled bleep. 'The last thing I said?'

'Yes, yes.'

'I said, you did ask for something seasonal. Why?'

'So these are *Christmas* angels, right?'

'Affirmative.'

'Then if the calendar reads nought, these angels are somehow involved in the very *first* Christmas!'

Arthur gave an impatient buzz. 'As I said, we are at the point in time from which we date the Christian calendar.' He buzzed again. 'Earl, you are uncharacteristically slow. Has that Christmas pudding gone to your head? I did warn you about a second helping.'

'Forget that,' snapped the astronaut. 'Just tell me exactly what *you* think is going on.'

'I thought it was obvious,' bleeped the computer. 'We are observing the angels assigned to annouce the arrival on earth of the Saviour – the Messiah, the Christ. If you check the co-ordinates for their flight path you'll see that their destination confirms this.'

Earl's eyes widened again. 'They're heading for – ?'

'Israel,' said Arthur. 'Or Judea as it's called at this time. Actually a small town known as Bethlehem.'

Earl's mouth fell open in total disbelief, his mind full of wonder. 'And I used to think all that Baby Jesus stuff was just a cosy little story – a sort of Christmas fairy-tale . . . '

Gentle lights flashed deep within the purple orb as Arthur double-checked his information. 'On the contrary,' he announced, 'the birth of Christ is well-documented in the holy book known as the Bible. That record, in the New Testament, is historically sound, as are the many references in the Old Testament. Some of these were written many hundreds of years before the event.'

'Hey, this is really something!' grinned the astronaut. 'Can we see for ourselves?'

'I'll check with Big Boy,' said Arthur, and after a brief electronic exchange with the master computer he bleeped the good news. 'Big Boy estimates that if we leave immediately in the shuttle-craft, and providing the heavenly host doesn't increase its speed, we should be able to touch down in the Judean hills a minute or two before they make their announcement to the shepherds.'

Earl gave a delighted whoop. 'What are we waiting for?'

Under cover of darkness the tiny two-man ship came in to land on vertical thrust (silent, of course, to save alarming the sheep) and settled gently in a grassy hollow.

'Are you sure this is the right spot?' questioned Earl as they climbed from the cockpit.

'My calculations show this to be the most likely place for the announcement,' Arthur assured him. 'My sensors show both human and animal life-forms just over this rise, and this group is the nearest to the town.'

Earl threw back his head and looked up into the night sky. 'No sign of the angels yet.'

'I think you'll find they've become invisible for the last stage of their journey,' said Arthur. 'According to the record their meeting with the shepherds is a fairly private affair. That is to say, they will appear suddenly and specifically to address these local stockmen.'

'Come on, then,' his master urged. 'I can't wait!'

But Earl did not have to wait, for it was exactly as he and his floating companion reached the top of the rise and caught sight of the shepherds gathered around a glowing fire that it happened. One moment it was a night like any other – cold, quiet and starlit – the next, these working men found themselves surrounded by a bright, phosphorescent glow, sharing their fire with a great, radiant being from another world.

'Incredible!' muttered Earl as he squatted down on the springy grass – but no sound came from the lips of the Judean shepherds. Fear had tied their tongues and it was all they could do to cower beneath the awesome glare.

But the angel reassured them, and through the tiny auto-interpreter Earl had pressed into his ear he heard the visitor say, 'Don't be afraid, lads. I bring you the best news you've ever heard, and it's good news for everyone. The Saviour – your long-awaited Messiah, the Lord – has been born tonight over in Bethlehem. You'll be able to recognize him, too – a baby lying in a manger.'

Then, as if by magic – though Earl suspected they had been there all the time awaiting their cue – the other angels appeared. They filled the sky – thousands of them in a stunning aerial spectacle – and they were singing in rapturous voices, 'Glory to God in highest heaven, and on earth peace, good will toward men.'

Earl could only stare, open-mouthed, not only because he had never seen such a sight or heard such music before, but because he was suddenly aware that this was a very special moment in the history of his world. It was somehow – what was the word? – *sacred*. As though he was on holy ground. Or for a moment had been lifted into heaven.

Trust Arthur to bring him down to earth! 'Very impressive,' he bleeped. 'I registered perfect vocal harmony with greater output than even the largest octophonic sound system.' Then he gave one of his electronic chuckles. 'Quite something for a singing telegram!'

Earl frowned at him. 'Arthur, this is no time to jest. This is a very special night for the human race.'

'I'm aware of that,' said the computer. 'I've just been running a check on all the references to this event in the Bible and it's plain that the arrival of the baby does indeed give cause for rejoicing. Which is probably why those stockmen are hurrying off towards the town.'

'What!' Earl turned quickly as the shepherds disappeared over the next rise. 'Come on, I've just gotta tag along. I *must* see him for myself.'

With Arthur at his side Earl headed across the hill and past the fire, following the shepherds. It didn't take them long to find the right place in the town. After hurrying down narrow streets, up rough-stone steps and through dark alleyways they came to what they thought was a likely place. The inn was doing a brisk trade this marrow-chilling night and their spokesman had to shout at the landlord to make himself heard.

A baby? Born in a manger? He knew nothing of such a scandal, but there *was* a young couple who had wanted lodgings. The inn was full, as was every other place in the town, so he had sent them round to bed down in the straw in an outhouse with the animals. But a *baby*? Well, yes, come to think of it, the woman did look as though she was expecting a baby. A young girl she was, bright-eyed and fresh-faced. Anyway, what did a bunch of shepherds want with a baby?

It was the long-awaited Saviour, they explained. Angels had appeared to them and told them where to find him.

The inn-keeper smothered a laugh. Poor fellows. The cold night-air had numbed their brains and they had started imagining things. Angels, indeed!

Watching from the doorway, Earl quickly stepped back into the shadows as the shepherds turned and came hurrying past him, still chattering excitedly. He motioned to Arthur to keep low, and together they followed at a distance. Round the side, through an alleyway, down some steps. And there it was – the actual setting of the Christmas story, a crude building visible in the moonlight and in the glow of a solitary oil-lamp that burned within. Yet it was nothing like the storybooks, and as Earl slowly approached and stood behind the shepherds now crowding on the threshold, his senses began to absorb the reality. The animals – cattle, donkeys and some oxen – had been crammed in with little room to move . . . the straw, soiled and left too long, smelled foul . . . and the young couple, still recovering from the trauma of delivering a baby unaided in such surroundings, sat weary and dishevelled . . .

Yet, as Earl crept nearer, he saw too the light of joy in the eyes of the young mother, the pride in the face of her man. With wonder he listened as one of the shepherds explained to Mary about the angels and as Joseph rose to his feet, intrigued by the spokesman's story. Yet Joseph was not surprised. He had known that the little one would cause a stir. He too had seen an angel and he knew that this baby would be different. Special.

But where *was* the baby? Earl stood on tiptoe and – there! The Christ-child. What a difference his arrival would make to the world.

The onlookers could only stand in silence now – the astronauts and the shepherds, divided by two thousand years of history, yet united in their common need of a Saviour, of someone like themselves who would show them the way to God.

Earl watched the baby's bright eyes and felt a smile rise from somewhere deep inside. Memories were coming to him, long-buried memories from his childhood, forgotten moments from a faraway Christmas. It had been a cold night just like this, but there was a warmth in the old chapel that seemed to come from somewhere other than the hot pipes running beneath the pews. It was a night of magic like this, too, because it had been a candlelight service and his young eyes had never before held the glow of a hundred tiny flames. And there had been singing – nothing to compare with those angels, of course – and Bible readings telling the Christmas story, and right at the front, beneath the tinsel-draped Christmas tree, there had been the manger scene – little model figures, a handful of straw, and a yellow bulb to make it glow. He remembered that now best of all. He had not been able to take his eyes off it, and at the close of the service he had rushed straight to that toy manger to look inside. To his disappointment something was missing.

'There's no baby Jesus,' he had complained to a round-faced woman who came to clear things away. 'You can't have Christmas without Jesus.'

But, as he had discovered every December since then, you could. And he had.

The shepherds stirred and he left his childhood memories behind. It was time to go. Earl looked once more into the tiny face in the hay and suddenly felt a compulsion to reach out and touch the Christ-child, if only to lay a finger on the back of his tiny hand. Yet as he reached forth he somehow knew this was not to be. There was no need. In some way that he did not understand, the Saviour had touched *him* . . .

Colonel Earl T. Parker awoke the following morning feeling abnormally light-headed. The events of the previous night came to him in a rush and he looked up from his bed, smiling. It was strange, though, that he could not remember the return journey with Arthur in the shuttle, or programming Big Boy to return them to his own time. He couldn't even recall changing into his sleep-suit before falling into bed.

He was still wondering about it when Arthur came floating in. 'Thank goodness you're awake, Earl,' bleeped the computer. 'Big Boy's complaining about someone tampering with his C1. Do come and sort him out.'

The astronaut looked up. 'What's that? Oh, sure, Arthur. But tell me something — did it really happen, or was I dreaming? Last night I mean — the baby and all that.'

Arthur bleeped impatiently. 'Can't we discuss it later, Colonel? Big Boy *is* in a mood.'

'OK. But fetch me some coffee, will you? And run the tapes for any messages. I want to know when they're sending that replacement.'

The computer buzzed in protest. 'Coffee, messages . . . next you'll be wanting me to clean your boots!'

'Boots?' said Earl, propping himself up on one elbow. 'What's wrong with my boots?'

Arthur buzzed again. 'Well, you can't go treading that straw all over the place! This is a space-station, not a farmyard.'

Earl scowled at the floating orb before glancing down at his boots lying on their side by the bed. Pieces of straw were sticking out from them, wedged between the ridges of the soles. Grinning, he reached down and plucked a straw free. 'Well, how d'you like that!' he beamed. 'It turned out to be quite a day after all.'

Arthur gave a long, chuckling bleep. 'Merry Christmas, Earl!'

Trapper's Trail

'Watch out for them grizzly bears. They can get awful mean in the spring.'

Those were the last words young Nick Bryce heard as the bush pilot dropped him off at Big Moose Lake deep in the Canadian backwoods, and they were the last words he expected to hear for another six weeks – the time he intended to spend alone trapping beaver in this remote part of British Columbia. As it was, he had hardly settled into the solitary cabin on the lake shore when another voice broke the wilderness silence.

'Hello-o? Anyone home?'

The voice sounded friendly enough, but as Nick turned from the log fire he was building he glanced quickly at his rifle by the door. With the weapon only a grab away, he opened up and stood looking out across the clearing to the big bearded figure dressed like himself in warm hunting clothes and carrying a bulging rucksack on his back. A powerful rifle hung from the stranger's shoulder and a long-bladed knife was strapped to his left boot. Nick thought he looked about twenty-eight years of age, ten years older than himself.

'Howdy,' Nick responded. 'What can I do for you?'

'Just passing,' the hunter replied, stepping forward. 'I saw your smoke from the trail up yonder and figured it would be good to see another face after all this time. Hope you don't mind.'

There was something about the man's smile that put Nick at ease. 'Not at all,' he said. 'I was just about to fix supper. You're welcome to join me. Stay overnight, too, if you like. There's plenty of room.'

The hunter grinned and reached behind him, pulling out a lifeless woodchuck. 'Can I add something to the pot? Shot this little fella just an hour back.'

'Sure.' Nick reached out his hand and introduced himself.

'Glad to meet you, Nick,' said the hunter. 'I'm Herb — Herb Ross — but my friends call me Gunner.'

The two men stepped inside the cabin and as they got talking Nick learned that Gunner's nickname had grown out of his love of hunting with a rifle, and the fact that his friends apparently thought he was a crack shot. For that reason he always got invited on hunting trips. But this time, just for once, Gunner was on his own.

'Sometimes I like to take off for these mountains, just to be by myself for a while,' he told Nick. 'I don't know about you, but I always feel closer to God out here; it's somewhere I can pray and think things through.'

Nick looked up from the food he was preparing, surprised. He hadn't figured Gunner for the sort of man who said his prayers. He was strong and burly with big, powerful hands — the type who could look after himself. Somehow Nick couldn't see such a man needing God's help, or asking for it — and anyway he didn't want to discuss it.

'Been out here long?' he asked.

'A couple of weeks,' Gunner replied. 'How about you?'

'Just arrived,' said Nick. 'I'll be here a few weeks — for the beaver. I guess you know the pelts are fetching a high price right now? I want to cash in on that to raise money for a business I plan to start. Refurbishing old autos — that sort of thing.'

Gunner nodded, studying Nick for a moment. 'Been in these parts before?'

'Sure. I've been here twice with my father. Mainly for

the trapping, but a bit of hunting and fishing, too.'

'This your first time on your own?'

'That's right,' said Nick, 'but it's no big deal. I know my way around.' There was a slight edge to his voice and Gunner backed off a little.

'I don't mean to intrude,' he said, 'but I know how cruel the wilderness can be. I lost a buddy out here about a year back.'

Nick's eyes widened. 'How d'you mean, lost him?'

'It was last spring,' said the hunter. 'We were camped just a few miles up the valley near Snakehead Point, hunting moose. But one morning I didn't feel too good and hung around camp while my partner, Jack Soames, went off on his own. I told him to watch out for himself but he just laughed and reminded me of all the big scouting awards he'd won.' He paused, looking out through the window to the wild world beyond. Then he turned to Nick. 'But he never came back.'

Nick stared at the big fellow for a moment. 'Well – what happened? Did they send out a search party?'

'Sure did,' said Gunner, 'but they didn't find a trace. He just vanished. The wilderness just swallowed him up.'

Nick was disturbed. 'But how could a guy like that fail to find his way out?'

Gunner shrugged. 'Who knows? They say these woods have eaten even some of the best trackers over the years. The backwoods are hundreds of miles square, you know that, and once a man starts to panic he begins to exhaust himself, and once he's exhausted he's as good as dead.'

Nick set down his knife, engrossed. 'Do you think that's what happened to your friend?'

'I figure he took a wrong turning at some crucial point that day,' Gunner explained, 'and from then on he got more and more lost.'

Lost. Out in the wilderness the word had a desperate

ring to it and Nick found himself shaking off a sudden shiver. Slightly unnerved, he turned his attention to the food.

Soon the two men were seated at the pine-plank table before the blazing log fire, eating their meal in the fading light of the wilderness evening. That finished, they cleared things away and pulled the cabin's hand-carved rocking chairs to the fire and sat, warmed by the glow of the logs, drinking hot, sweet coffee. The cabin was lit by a solitary kerosene lamp, and for a while they talked of their families and hometowns. Nick was from Salter's Rise, a farming community about three hundred miles south-east. Gunner came from Alterton, just 120 miles due south and the nearest town. It was from there, he told Nick, that he and Jack Soames had flown out to Snakehead Point by helicopter just a few weeks short of a year ago. It seemed Gunner couldn't get away from the hunting trip that had gone wrong, and much as Nick would have preferred a different conversation, he somehow found himself drawn to the details of the tragedy with a strange fascination.

'I guess there's not a lot anyone can do once they're lost in these mountains,' said Nick.

Gunner agreed. 'A man could walk for weeks on end and still not find his way out. Yet, the way I see it, there is something you could do.' He looked squarely at Nick. 'In a tight spot a man could pray.'

Nick laughed shortly. 'You know, you sound like my grandmother. She's always going on about God wanting to guide me. "Just turn to him in prayer, Nick," she says. "No one loves you and wants to help you more than the Good Lord." But I don't go for that stuff. I've got a brain and a pair of hands − I can find my own way.'

Gunner leaned back in his chair, nodding thoughtfully. 'I admire your spirit, Nick, but no man's so tough or clever that he doesn't need help at some time or other. And me, I never set foot in these mountains before I ask the Lord's help and protection.'

'Oh? And what about your buddy who got lost?'

Gunner met Nick's eyes. 'I can't speak for Jack. And I don't pretend to know all the answers, neither. All I know is, Jack Soames was one of the finest trackers I ever knew — and when it came to the crunch that wasn't enough.'

Nick had nothing to say to that and he fell silent, gazing into the fire. Then Gunner went on, 'See that text up there?'

Nick followed his eyes to the faded tapestry hanging above the fireplace. The needlework had long lost its vivid colours, but the wording was still clear. *In all thy ways acknowledge Him, and He shall direct thy paths.*

'What about it?'

'That's a line from the Bible,' Gunner told him. 'Means a lot to me. I first heard it years ago in a little tent mission that came to town, and I've never forgotten it. I guess it's a sort of formula I've adopted — each morning when I rise I put myself into God's hands. Sure have felt the benefit of it.' He smiled to himself. 'It's so simple. And God is faithful. Yes, I reckon those words have kept me from quite a few scrapes . . . '

The big man let the sentence hang in the air like the traces of smoke escaping from the log fire, but Nick did not ask him to go on. He really didn't want to know. Gunner Ross was a strange mixture, he decided. Surely a *real* man could find his way through life without having to rely on some sort of religious idea? 'No,' said Nick at last, 'I don't need any help.'

Gunner smiled resignedly and leaned forward to throw another log on the fire. 'Well, take care out there in the wilds, anyway.'

Nick forced a smile, a little irritated. 'I know what I'm

96

doing. I know where the beaver are and I know the paths. Nothing's going to happen to me. Besides, I have to make it back home to start my business. I've got big plans, remember?'

Gunner had nothing to say to that, and before long they threw their sleeping-bags down on the cabin's crude wooden bunks and turned in. Both wanted an early start in the morning, and with the warmth of the fire, and the gentle night sounds of the wilderness, they were soon being lulled into sleep.

When Nick awoke next morning he was alone. His visitor had gone and the cabin now felt cold and somehow empty. Though he had failed to understand the man called Gunner he had quite liked him and was aware of just how much he would miss companionship during the long weeks that lay ahead of him. 'Nothing to be done about it, though,' he told himself, and soon he set to packing his rucksack for the day's trapping. After a simple breakfast he headed out into the wilderness.

Over the years, Nick Bryce had learned a great deal about trapping from his father and from the start his plans went smoothly. His only disappointment was that the most beaver were to be found farther north than he had expected, which meant he had to walk many more miles than he had intended. After two weeks he located an area where the beaver were plentiful and decided to move his base from the cabin to a small storm-shelter much nearer his trapping ground. In this way he saved himself several hours of legwork each day and began to collect pelts at what he judged to be a very lucrative rate. By the end of four weeks he had amassed almost fifty skins, cached in two principal stores. After the fifth week, with a tally of more than sixty-five pelts, he decided to finish trapping and spend the remaining days of his stay cleaning the skins and transferring them south to the cabin ready for his departure in the bush-plane.

But getting them there was going to take a lot longer than Nick had originally planned. Because of the weight of the pelts he was forced to plan three journeys, beginning with the smaller quantity of skins which he had cached twelve miles north of Big Moose Lake. A second, heavier pack of skins − a 40lb load − had to be retrieved from almost sixteen miles away, and in addition to the pelts he had a rucksack containing all the equipment he had brought with him − sleeping-bag, rifle, ammunition, axe, and food supplies. It was this punishing weight on his second journey that persuaded him to abandon the familiar track after eight miles in order to find a more direct route back. He saw no problem with this. He knew exactly where he was and his compass would enable him to cut across country and knock hours off the long walk to the cabin. To make sure he made no mistake he stopped frequently to check his bearings and to correct his route.

After many hours, however, Nick emerged from the underbrush to find himself in a pass he did not recognize. Slipping the now crushing weights from his back, he slumped down on an old tree stump and wondered where he could be. For a long time he sat looking out at the unfamiliar view. He checked his compass once more and glanced at the sky for confirmation of north, but leaden clouds had rolled in and it was impossible to figure his exact position.

At last, after resting and eating just a little of the food he carried with him, he pulled on his loads and set off again, heading down the pass on the remains of what had once been a beaten track. This direction he chose by instinct, sensing that he had somehow come too far west. He needed to go south-east, he decided, and this overgrown path would take him that way.

An hour later the light began to fade and he still had not recognized any feature of the landscape. 'Best to hole up for the night,' he told himself. 'Make a fresh start in the morning.' And with that he dropped his packs, crawled into his sleeping-bag and fell fast asleep.

The new morning brought hope and renewed energy. A clear sky confirmed that he was travelling in the right direction, and after a light breakfast Nick drew on his loads and set out resolutely for the cabin.

But he did not reach it that day, nor the next, and on the following day, several miles to the east – that was as near as he could judge – he heard the buzz of the bush-plane that was flying in to pick him up from Big Moose Lake.

Until that moment he had managed to keep his fears at bay. Now a cold terror shot through him and he fought to control himself. 'It'll be all right,' he muttered. 'As long as you don't panic, it'll be all right.'

It was another hour before he heard the plane again, still miles to the east, and he realized the pilot must have waited some time before deciding that his passenger wasn't going to show up. As the noise of the plane died away, Nick stared up at the sky, fighting the fear that loomed with the realization that he had been left behind – and that he was lost.

Trembling, he sank down on a boulder and shrugged off his loads. He would not panic, he told himself, he would not give in. 'You're going to make it,' he kept muttering. 'It'll take time, but you're going to make it.'

The key to survival, he knew, lay in the mind. All he had to do was keep his head and cover as much ground as possible each day without over-stretching himself.

He sat trying to gather his thoughts. There was nothing to be gained by trying to find the cabin now –

that would only waste time. His new route must lie to the south and his goal would be Alterton, the town Gunner had said was 120 miles away. At least he could be thankful for that information. He had a goal, something he could work towards every day. He could make it.

He drew his rucksack towards him and took stock of his supplies. Food would be his biggest problem. He had only one normal day's provisions left, but he would make that last three or four days and try to supplement his meals with what he could kill – a grouse or woodchuck, or even a snake. He checked his ammunition. Fifteen shells. Not enough, he thought, considering he was not a particularly good shot, but maybe sufficient for him to get by. He would have to make every round count.

He turned his attention to the pelts and sat looking at them, reliving the little dream he had nursed of setting himself up in business. This was no time for regrets, though. The pelts would have to go. There was now only one skin worth saving, and that was his own.

Glancing at the sun, he stood and faced south, staring into the trackless forest that stretched out before him. Pulling on his rucksack, he moved forward.

It was hard work each step of the way. When he wasn't climbing up one hill or slithering precariously down another, he was hacking his way through dense underbrush or stumbling across a shallow creek. It was as though the whole of nature conspired to sap his strength, pummel his spirits, and force him into the same submission that had been the death of others who had lost their way.

At least, he thought, the elements were on his side. But a day later, as though in mocking response, thunderclouds came growling in from the east and unleashed a howling storm. Burrowing deep into the undergrowth, he sought out a natural shelter and settled inside his sleeping-bag to wait it out. The rain fell for three days.

When at last Nick emerged he was weak from lack of food and as a result squandered several of his few remaining shells in pursuit of fresh meat. He bagged only one small woodchuck.

After two weeks he was beginning to feel the effects of his ordeal. Insufficient food, constant strenuous activity and blistered feet were taking their toll. His clothes were ripped and shredded by the continual snagging of trees and brush, his hands and face had been scratched by a million thorns, and he was losing weight by the day. Each evening he collapsed into his sleeping-bag knowing he could not go on. Yet each morning he rose determined to reach civilization.

Towards the end of the third week as he sat on a boulder looking out across a valley at some magnificent mountain scenery, he told himself that if he was to keep going he must have more food. He checked his ammunition and found that he was down to five shells – nowhere near enough to see him out of this green-tangled hell. He would have to eat more vegetation. He had already been eating berries and shoots that he knew were harmless; now it was time to try other sources. Leaves, roots, bulbs, seeds – he knew there were many natural foods all around him, but everything would need to be carefully tested. He could not afford to fall ill or that would be the end of him. Meanwhile he resorted to what he believed to be a reliable standby – the inner bark of trees. He knew that this could be boiled, roasted or eaten raw, and he remembered reading somewhere that the only exceptions were those barks that had a bitter taste.

At least he was getting enough water, he reflected. The wilderness was running with creeks and streams, thanks to the thawing winter snows on higher ground, and by careful rationing of water from the flask he carried he was able to avoid adding dehydration to his problems. As the days dragged on he began to feel unwell. An increased diet of bark, berries and leaves had not given him the nourishment he needed and his strength was slipping away. He craved meat, but because his hands were now shaky and his eyesight dim, he did not think he would be able to shoot anything as small as a grouse. And larger game did not come his way. On some days he tried fishing, but he caught nothing at all and was forced back to eating vegetation.

On his thirty-fifth night lost in the wilderness he lay in his sleeping-bag and thought about Jack Soames, the confident, experienced woodsman who had walked off into the wilderness in search of moose, never to be heard of again. How *could* it happen, especially when the man must have had a reliable compass? But then, how had it happened to *him*? In a moment of blind panic he wondered how long Jack Soames had lasted before the wilderness won? And as for his own fate . . .

He checked himself. 'You're going to make it,' he told himself sternly. 'However long it takes.'

Lying beneath the stars, wishing for sleep but unable to slow his racing mind, his thoughts went to Gunner Ross. How would *he* have coped? he wondered. Yet he knew the answer to that. Gunner would have prayed.

He shook his head, resisting the thought. 'Religious mumbo-jumbo,' he said aloud. It was a phrase he had used before, and with his mind in overdrive he heard his grandmother gently rebuking him. 'Now, now, Nick, there's no call for that. You can't criticize prayer until you've tried it.'

In a daze of fatigue and drowsiness, he remembered arguing with her. 'But I'm not likely to try it − I don't have cause to pray.'

'Well, maybe one day you will,' she had said. 'Then

you'll find out for yourself.'

He awoke the next morning and pushed on. By now his clothes were rags flying in the spring breeze about his wasted body. He had lost more than 30lb in weight. He had no idea how far he had travelled nor how much further he had to go before he reached civilization. All he was sure of was his general direction. If only he could come across some landmark, some feature of these cruel backwoods that would confirm his progress and cheer him on. But there was nothing – until days later he reached the river: a broad torrent of a river flowing east to west. Of course! He had seen this river from the air each time he had flown in to Big Moose Lake. It was an early feature of the wilderness only five or six minutes in from the first crop of trees that marked the beginning of the backwoods. Now, here it was, running cool and clear before his eyes and only a day or two from the outside world. He was nearly free! He was going to make it!

But then the daunting truth hit him. The river, running deep and icy-cold, might be the very thing that would prevent him from reaching the civilization it promised him. How could he cross it?

He sank down on the ground, dejected. This river ran eastwards for miles; there was no telling how long he would have to follow its course before he found a crossing-place. And there was no way he could swim it – the current was far too strong and would almost certainly sweep him to his death. He dropped his head into his hands. Had he come all this way just to drown?

He sat for a long time trying to marshall his thoughts. There *had* to be a way. Soon it came to him. It was so simple, really. All he had to do was fell one of the towering pine trees that grew along the river bank and walk across. Surely these trees were tall enough to reach to the other side? Rallying his now fading strength, he reached into his rucksack for the axe and went to work.

It was a long job. He was in his seventh week at the mercy of the wilderness and he didn't possess the stamina for such heavy exercise. Yet he persevered, careful to make every blow with the axe count. But when at last the tree fell, his spirits toppled with it. The pine was too short and was carried swiftly downstream and out of sight.

Exhausted and disillusioned, he leaned against a tree and cursed his fate, wondering whether he should admit defeat and let the wilderness have its way. Was it really worth trying to go on?

But the thought had barely formed before he was back on his feet, his heart pounding, his instinct for survival never more keen as it sent waves of panic surging through his body. There were noises coming from within the dark wood – threatening noises that were moving nearer.

'Grizzly!' he muttered, peering into the dense underbrush, but he saw no movement. Then, as in a nightmare, it was suddenly in front of him, nine feet tall and a massive thousand pounds in weight, its claws outstretched to kill.

Summoning strength he didn't know he had, he sprang for the rifle and snatched it up, knowing it was loaded. Just one bullet – that was all he would have time to use.

Raising the weapon to his shoulder, he took aim as the giant bear trampled towards him. Shakily, his finger squeezed on the trigger – but his eye would not focus and the bear seemed to be swaying about in his sights. Shudders of fear went racing through him and perspiration streamed down his face. Desperate, he fired – and missed by a yard.

He cursed aloud and hurled the rifle at the creature, but it kept coming towards him. As he backed away,

Nick glanced around. No way out. He was up against the river and he was trapped.

The bear came at him swiftly now, towering over him and slashing the air with those murderous claws. Trembling, he took a pace backwards, his foot plunging into ice-cold water. 'Oh, God!' he cried. 'Help me!'

The sharp crack of a rifle spliced the cool air. The bear roared, whined, then staggered and fell, crashing to the stony ground only three paces from where Nick was standing. Shaking with fright, and terribly confused, he whirled around. Who had fired the . . . ?

'Gunner!'

He saw the woodsman wave and smile from across the river as he lowered the rifle, but suddenly everything was swaying – the trees, the river, the mountains . . . Then he was falling, swooning as he went, and as he hit the ground he caught sight of the lifeless bear. Distant words surfaced in his mind and he was hearing the warning of the bush pilot. 'Watch out for them grizzly bears,' the man had said. 'They can get awful mean in the spring.'

It had been an incredible piece of shooting, he mused.

Then, on his forty-eighth day in the wilderness, he passed out and his world went black.

'You've had a very lucky escape, son.'

Nick nodded and tried to smile, but only tears would come. He had been in the hospital three days now and this was the first morning that he had been fully conscious. Slowly he was recovering from malnutrition, shock, and acute fatigue. His bearded face, gaunt features and wasted body told their own story.

His father sat by the bed as he had done since he had first been called the night Nick had been admitted. There had, of course, been an official search party but when they failed to find Nick, his father had all but given up hope of seeing his son alive again. Sitting by his bedside, he could still scarcely believe it.

The doctor spoke again. 'Yes, I'd say you're extremely lucky. There are not many men who get lost in those woods and come out alive. You've a lot to be thankful for.'

Nick nodded again, aware that the doctor was right, but it was another two days before he could talk about his ordeal without tears springing from his eyes and emotion choking his voice. 'I don't even know how it happened,' he told his father. 'I used my compass all the time when I was trying to find a shorter route back to the cabin.'

His father smiled gently and shook his head. 'Nick, don't you remember me telling you about the mineral deposits up in those mountains – how they can deflect a compass and throw a man off course? That's probably what made you go wrong that first afternoon.'

Nick frowned. 'Why didn't I think of that? That's exactly what must have happened. What a fool I was.'

'Well, don't blame yourself, son. I guess it could happen to anyone. A man can only follow the paths he believes to be right.'

'Paths?' Nick looked up at his father as words tumbled about in his brain, and soon he had the phrase he was looking for. '*In all thy ways acknowledge Him, and He shall direct thy paths.*'

His father only heard him muttering and smiled benignly. He had been told that Nick's thinking might be muddled for a while and he must be prepared to ignore any ramblings.

'We'll talk about it when you're fit again, son. Don't let it worry you now. Just concentrate on getting your strength back, that's all that matters. Then, when you get home, we can talk about that business you wanted to start.'

'But, Dad, I – '

'And don't worry about the money. I know you wanted to make it on your own, but as things haven't worked out I'm going to cash in an insurance policy and let you have the proceeds to get you established.'

Nick smiled. 'I appreciate that, Dad, but right now I'm not even sure that I want to start that business – or that I'm meant to. You see, something happened to me up in those mountains and – '

'I'll say it did!' This was a new voice, though Nick recognized it even before he turned.

'Gunner!'

The big man smiled. 'Thought I'd drop in to see how you were doing.'

Nick reached out a hand. 'I owe you a great deal, Gunner. What can I say but – thanks!'

'And I'd like to add my thanks to that, Mr Ross,' said Nick's father, getting to his feet. 'The family's deeply grateful to you.'

Gunner shrugged. 'I'm just glad I was around when I was needed.'

'That's something I've been wondering about,' said Nick. 'How you happened to be right there when that grizzly was about to finish me off.'

The trapper nodded. 'That's an interesting story. You see, for several weekends I'd been going up to the mountains to look for you, even though the official search had been called off. I had a strong feeling you were still alive, against all the odds, so I kept on looking – until last weekend. By then I was beginning to wonder whether I'd been wasting my time and I was planning to go visit my folks in Vancouver. But all the while I was packing my case I felt I really ought to be getting my rucksack ready again, so I followed that instinct and set out for the wilderness one more time.'

'I'm sure glad you did,' said Nick. 'But how did you

find me? How did you know where to look?'

'I didn't,' Gunner confessed. 'But the Lord knew where you were, so I just asked him to guide my steps and show me. I guess that's what he did.'

Nick nodded, his eyes bright. 'It's that Bible verse of yours, isn't it?'

'You've got it,' Gunner smiled.

'Bible verse?' said Nick's father. 'What verse?'

His son turned to face him, a grin spreading across his gaunt face. 'It's something Gunner taught me that first night up in the cabin, Dad – something I'm not likely to forget in a long, long time. And, you know what, it's something Grandma's been trying to teach me for years. It goes like this . . . '

The Legend
of Gloom Valley

Michael stood looking up at the mountain – what he could see of it through the swirling grey mist – then turned to go back inside the *Gasthaus*. There was still no one about so he struggled out of his rucksack and went and warmed himself by the crackling log fire. Staring down into the flames he found himself yawning. It had been a long and tiring walk from the station and he wished he'd accepted that offer of a lift. Or maybe the sudden warmth was to blame.

'You have been waiting long?'

He turned as a plump, balding man came bustling through a side door, his arms full of long, snow-brushed logs.

'Not long,' said Michael. 'Besides, I'm in no hurry.'

'Who *is* around here?' laughed the man as he dropped the logs beside the huge fireplace. He picked up two of them and tossed them into the flames. 'Around here there is nothing to hurry for. You want a room?'

'Just somewhere to lay my head. I expect you're pretty busy at this time of year?'

The plump man waddled to the desk and turned the register round. 'Does it look as if I'm busy? Do you see guests rushing through the lobby? Visitors falling over one another for a room?' He laughed again. 'Gloom Valley is never busy, my friend. Thanks to the cloud. The cloud and the mountain.'

Michael picked up the pen and signed his name. They had warned him about this place. But then he'd never been able to refuse a challenge. 'I've not heard it called

Gloom Valley before. I don't think it'll do much for your tourist industry.'

The man shrugged his shoulders and reached for a key. 'What tourist industry? No holiday brochure could persuade people to flock to this place. Who wants a holiday without sunshine?'

'Surely you get your share? Every place has its off-days.'

The man's eyes were sad. 'Here every day is an off-day. Only some days are worse than others. If you are lucky, like today, you get just the cloud. But tomorrow . . . who knows how fierce a blizzard may come sweeping down the valley? Now, the next village on from here gets plenty of sunshine and – '

'I didn't come here for the sun,' Michael said, a little impatient. 'I came here for the mountain.'

The man stared at him. 'Then I must ask you to pay for your room in advance.'

Michael smiled. 'Is it really that dangerous? I *have* climbed mountains before, including some of the toughest.'

The man nodded, studying Michael's fresh face. 'You are too young.'

'To climb mountains? Oh, come on.'

'Too young to die,' said the man. 'That mountain is a killer, my friend. It will eat you alive. Take my advice and go skiing, or visit the ice caves and take nice photographs, but don't risk your young neck on that . . . that monster.'

Michael fought off another smile. 'Can you tell me where to find a guide?'

'Sure. Just outside the village – the cemetery is full of them.'

The young man let out a hoot of laughter. 'You're kidding me, surely? There must be a guide.'

'Oh yes, there is one. Old Franz. He will tell you all

you want to know. But don't ask him to climb with you. He got wise before he got dead.'

Michael picked up the key and tossed it in the air. 'Where do I find him?'

'He'll be here tonight, in the bar as usual. Buy him an ale and he'll tell you the whole story.'

'The story?'

The plump man closed the register. 'The legend. Ha! Once you get him on that subject you'll never get him off it. Just ask him about the legend of Gloom Valley.'

Michael went early to the bar – just half an hour after it had opened – but already it was packed. Mostly local people, he thought, with just a handful of outsiders. Even so, an old guide ought to be easy to spot. Was that him, the wiry figure sitting in an easy chair beside the fire? He went and bought two tankards of ale and squeezed through the crowd, his eyes smarting at the tobacco smoke.

'Excuse me, are you Franz?'

The old man looked up. 'Which Franz do you want? Voight, Schmidt, Kronig?'

'The guide,' Michael explained.

The old man chuckled. 'That's me. Sit down, young man. Though I must warn you I am not for hire. I gave all that up long ago.'

'I realize that. I just wanted to talk.' He held out a tankard and the old guide took it.

'I'll talk with any man who buys me ale,' he said. 'What do you want to know?'

Michael settled into a chair and set down his tankard. 'About the mountain.'

Franz nodded, running his bony fingers through his white hair. 'It figures,' he said, a little wearily. 'Every stranger I meet wants to climb the mountain. And I tell them all the same thing: don't bother – it's better to stay alive. And you – you are so young. Why do you want to throw your life away? How old are you, anyway?'

'Eighteen. But I've had a lot of experience. I did the Eiger last spring.'

The old man seemed impressed. 'North face?'

'On my own.'

Franz touched his forelock, smiling. 'I salute you, young man. I was twenty-three. Of course, that was a good few years ago. Seems like a dream to me now . . . '

'But what about *this* mountain?' Michael asked. 'You *have* climbed it?'

The old man's face darkened. 'Climbed it, yes. But not conquered it. No man has conquered it, my boy. It's just not possible.'

Michael grinned. 'The unclimbable mountain? Isn't that just a myth?'

Franz sipped his ale. 'Eighty-three deaths is no myth. Surely you don't want to become the eighty-fourth?'

Michael thought about it. 'Someone has to prove it can be done.'

'Oh, someone will – but, with respect, I somehow doubt that it will be you. You don't strike me as being of royal blood. Besides, you're not from these parts.'

Michael stared at the old guide. 'What do you mean, royal blood? What are you talking about?'

'It's in the legend,' Franz said.

Michael nodded slowly. Of course. 'Tell me about the legend.'

'Well, that will take some telling,' the old man smiled, glancing at his tankard.

'All right, I'll get more ale. Just give me a minute.'

Soon Michael was back with a tray of three large tankards. 'All for you,' he said. 'Will that keep you going?'

Franz laughed. 'Well, if you have all evening, so have I. Now where to begin?' He shifted in his seat and turned to gaze into the fire, remembering. 'The old legend goes back a long way – how far no one knows – to a time when the mountain was owned by a king who lived in a palace built among the highest peaks. Once a year, says the legend, the King came down into the valley to hold a grand party for his people. And anyone who cared to make the climb – there was a safe, easy route then – they were welcome in the King's court. At that time, of course, it was a happy valley with contented people. They loved their king, were well cared for by him, and to complete their joy they had permanent sunshine.' He turned to the young mountaineer. 'Sounds like a fairy tale, yes? But let me go on.'

He told Michael that, according to the legend, this happy state of affairs had not lasted. One of the King's courtiers, a man of very high office, had become jealous of his master's position and plotted to overthrow the throne. He was found out at the last minute, however, and expelled from the palace. Thereafter he had lived in the mountains where he spent his energies in frustrating all communication between the palace and the people. He had done his worst, Franz said, when he destroyed part of an important bridge – a rock formation over a narrow abyss. Without that bridge the King could no longer come down into the valley, and the people could no longer ascend to the palace. A little while later a terrible avalanche had covered the mountain path.

Michael listened intently. 'But why couldn't the King get the bridge repaired?' he asked.

'It wasn't for lack of trying,' the old guide replied. 'You see, the exiled servant developed strong and mysterious powers which he used against anyone who tried to restore the bridge. Some were just beaten off or frightened away; others – many others – were killed, hurled to their death down the abyss.'

'But couldn't the King's Guard catch this rebel and

put an end to all the trouble?'

Franz nodded. 'They tried, of course, but the servant was able to change himself into rock or ice and become part of the landscape. Such a man was impossible to catch. And then there was the appalling weather — the black cloud which had enveloped the mountain peaks ever since the bridge had been destroyed. The same cloud, they say, that hangs over the mountain and blocks the sun from the valley to this very day.'

'So the *Gastwirtin* was right — that you don't get any sun here.'

'That part of the legend I can vouch for,' said Franz. 'Occasionally we get a glimpse of the sun first thing in the morning, but that cloud keeps us in shadow the rest of the time. It has always been that way.'

Michael nodded. 'So the mountain is said to be unclimbable because this character with the strange powers is supposed to be up there to this day, throwing mountaineers into the abyss?'

Franz noted the smile in Michael's eyes. 'You can laugh if you wish, young man, but yes, that is what the legend says.'

'And you believe it?'

The old man shrugged. 'All I know for sure is that many good men — experienced mountaineers — have lost their lives in those peaks, and that a good number of them died in the abyss.'

'But what about yourself?' Michael persisted. 'You say you've climbed the mountain. How far did you get? And why couldn't you complete the ascent? Did *you* come across the enemy?'

'Questions, questions,' said the old man. 'Will you slow up a little?' He swigged his ale. 'Yes, I've climbed the mountain, but only the once, when I was not much older than you. Most of the men in the valley have tried at some time or other, and those who haven't either

114

given up or fallen off have wound up dead.'

'What happened to you, then? Did you give up?'

'No such thing, young man. Before you reach the broken bridge there's a tricky ice-wall – an ascent of about two hundred feet. My partner, climbing ahead of me, had just reached the top of this when I heard him cry out – a shriek of horror. Then all was silent. Suddenly I was falling through space. I dropped over a thousand feet and was lucky to escape with broken legs. When they showed me the rope I realized it had been cut – hacked through with an ice-axe in one blow.'

Michael's eyes widened and the colour drained from his face. 'The servant?' he gasped.

The old climber smiled, teasing his young listener for a moment. 'Well, it certainly wasn't my friend. They found his body at the bottom of the abyss a week later.'

Michael stared at the old guide for long moments, then gulped down his ale. 'Is that all there is to the legend?'

Franz nodded. 'Almost, anyway. For years after the bridge was first broken nothing was heard from the King's courts and the people here began to wonder whether their ruler was even still alive. But then they say that one day a royal eagle swooped out of the sky and dropped a scroll bearing the King's seal. That scroll simply stated that the King had not forgotten his people and that at some time in the future a member of the royal line would himself come and repair the broken bridge and deal with the servant once and for all, thus opening up the way to the palace again.' He paused, looking Michael in the eye. 'That's what I meant about royal blood. We're still waiting for him, you see. The legend says that once he arrives and restores the bridge the cloud will disappear and we shall be able to see the sun again.'

'*And* the palace,' Michael ventured.

Old Franz laughed. 'So you believe the legend?'

'I believe I'd like to climb the mountain,' Michael said. 'The only reservation I have is that − '

He did not finish for at that moment a hush fell upon the room, as though something of great importance was about to happen. Michael looked at Franz for some explanation but the old guide just shrugged. It was then they felt the icy blast from across the room and realized that the door to the street was open. Intrigued, Michael stood to see what was happening, just in time to watch a big man enter amidst a flurry of snow.

Closing the door behind him, the stranger turned to face all the staring eyes, a tall, muscular figure with full beard and a flowing mane of hair hanging down around his shoulders. Even through the crowd Michael could see that he was dressed for climbing.

'Good evening,' said the stranger. 'I'm looking for someone to tackle the mountain with me.'

There was a moment's pause before the silence gave way to a burst of laughter. 'Just another crazy mountaineer!' someone called, and one by one the patrons turned their backs on him.

Michael looked down at Franz. 'Will you excuse me?'

The old guide chuckled. 'Watch out for that ice-wall, won't you?'

Michael smiled, then pushed his way through the crowd to where the stranger was hanging up his waterproofs. 'Can I buy you a drink?' he asked, lifting the man's bulging rucksack into a corner.

The bearded face turned. 'I'd like that, thank you. Something to warm me through; it's bitter out there tonight.'

'But the weather should hold for a day or two, if you're thinking of climbing.'

The stranger smiled and together they crossed to the bar. 'And you? You're climbing too?'

'With you, if that's all right,' Michael said boldly. He

116

glanced around at the disinterested crowd. 'In fact, I don't think you'll get any other offers tonight.'

The man laughed and reached out his hand. 'I'd be glad to have you along. What do I call you?'

'Michael. And you?'

'I am known as The Lion,' he said, tossing back his great mane of hair. 'That's what they call me in the palace, anyway.'

Across the room a man almost choked on his brandy.

A small crowd had gathered outside the *Gasthaus* to see them off, well-wishers standing side by side with hecklers in the still morning air. Old Franz stood on the verandah watching the climbers pack the last of their things into rucksacks and then turned his eyes to the mountain. Somehow nothing had ever stirred his memories so deeply as what he was witnessing right now and he found himself fighting to keep the lump from his throat. 'It was a morning just like this . . . ' he muttered. And when at last they waved their goodbye and set off down the snow-muffled street it was *his* voice above all others that Michael heard. 'May the King be with you,' he was calling – which was a very strange thing, for no one in the valley had heard those words in a long, long time.

Soon they had turned the last corner and were heading out over the fields, down beside the frozen lake and across the little timber bridge. Here the overgrown pathway swung steeply upwards, twisting first this way then that until they were treading the fallen shingle of a thousand tiny avalanches.

On a bright, sunlit morning, Michael mused, such exercise would be bracing. But in some way that he did not understand the black cloud above them would not permit such thoughts. It was an angry cloud, dark and menacing, the likes of which he had never seen before;

a cloud that seemed unnervingly alive; a cloud that from time to time would grunt its disapproval of their mission through rumbling thunder.

'No wonder they call it Gloom Valley,' Michael called out as his partner hammered in the first pitons of the climb.

The Lion looked down, grinning. 'We'll see if we can't change that, yes?'

Michael could only nod, not knowing what to make of this powerful man with the strange name. Who was he, really? And where had he come from? That nonsense about the palace and the old legend was all very well for a fireside story, but what was the truth of the matter?

Yet these were only fleeting thoughts; climbing demanded concentration. Even though it was the man above who was choosing the route and positioning the pitons, the belaying-rope that joined them meant that both had to take equal care: either could fall and drag the other to his death.

But they were climbing well together. The teamwork necessary for a successful ascent came to them quickly, Michael responding skilfully to the evident expertise of his guide. There was no hesitating with this man. Whatever was called for − strategically-placed pitons or steps cut into the ice − The Lion acted decisively, as though he knew the mountain better than the back of his hand. Was this his secret? Michael wondered. Had he in fact scaled these treacherous walls before?

By mid-afternoon, with thousands of feet behind them, they were well into the second stage of the ascent and able to glance down at what now appeared as a toy-town village − tiny clusters of homes littering the valley floor.

Looking upwards was less inspiring. Towering high above them the great ridges of rock and ice teetered one upon another, defiantly clambering ahead of them and disappearing into the awful swirling mists that Michael knew would make their hazardous ordeal even more risky.

But such diversions had to be only momentary. One wrong move and they could part company with the rock-face for good. Besides, the weather was beginning to turn and an icy wind was plucking at their clothes and numbing their gloved fingers. It was a battle now – a battle to stay on the mountain and to find shelter for the night before the fading light robbed them of the chance. Yet Michael never doubted that the man above him had this in hand.

It was then that The Lion turned and shouted something to him, but his voice was snatched away on the wind. Michael shook his head, gesturing helplessly with one hand, and The Lion turned again, pointing upwards with his ice-pick to an overhanging rock jutting from the face about a hundred feet above them. Michael nodded his approval. It seemed the only place of shelter within their reach.

A furious wind was whistling around them as The Lion reached down to help Michael up into the small niche that was to be their home for the night.

'If we press as far back as we can into the rock we shall be out of the main blast,' The Lion explained, reaching into his rucksack. He pulled out a leather flask and handed it to his young companion. 'Brandy. It will help keep out the cold.'

Michael took it gratefully and swallowed two big mouthfuls, sensing the warmth flooding his stomach almost immediately. He smiled his appreciation, returning the flask. 'How about something to eat? I've plenty here.' He dragged his rucksack nearer to him, and soon they were eating in silence, huddled together for warmth and staring out into the darkness. Only once did Michael attempt to ease forward and peer down at the tiny twinkling lights of the village far below them.

'You climb well,' said The Lion.

'You are a good guide,' Michael replied, hesitating with the question on his lips. But then it was out. 'You've climbed her before?'

'I know the mountain well,' was all the bearded man would say.

'So you reckon we'll make it?'

There was no hesitation. 'I came to conquer, Michael, and that's what I'm going to do.'

The younger man couldn't resist a smile. 'Is that just plain grit, or do you know something that I don't?'

'I cannot fail,' said The Lion. 'It has been determined by royal decree.'

Michael fell silent. Could that legend possibly be true? But the question did not occupy him for long. Within a very short time, to the sound of the wind beating around the peaks and the occasional clatter of small stones tumbling past them, Michael was asleep.

He awoke in the broad light of day, thankful that the wind had retreated with the darkness, and vaguely conscious of the aroma of coffee. A moment later The Lion was pressing a hot mug into his hand. Michael mumbled his thanks and eased himself into an upright position, feeling his numbed body protesting at sleeping awkwardly on a bed of rock.

But soon they were moving again, climbing slowly at first as they worked off the stiffness of their cramped sleep, and then building up their speed to the expert pace of the previous day. Within an hour they were at the foot of the ice-wall.

Breathing heavily, Michael eased himself on to the ledge where his companion stood looking up at what they both knew would be the most dangerous part of the climb.

'Like a frozen waterfall,' said the big man. He turned to Michael. 'If you want to turn back now's the time.'

The young climber ignored the remark and slammed his pick into the ice. 'Seems firm enough. But that mist up there isn't going to help.'

The real hazard on Michael's mind, however, was one that he could not bring himself to mention. Had old Franz's fall from this same ice-wall really been an act of attempted murder? And if so, was that same enemy lying in wait for them both even now? But that was foolishness, he told himself, and he pushed the thought from his mind, settling to the climb.

Considering the risks on this phase of the ascent he was surprised at the speed with which The Lion was working – almost as though he was in a hurry to reach the top. Yet his swiftness was not at the expense of their safety. There was a measured certainty about each of the pitons the man drove home – two at each stage: one for a foot-hold, the other for securing the rope with a snap-link – and Michael confidently followed behind feeling unreasonably safe. It was an extraordinary thing: their ascent of this ice-wall was probably the most dangerous piece of mountaineering he had ever tackled, yet with The Lion in front of him he felt perfectly secure. Why should that be?

And then, quite uninvited, another thought dropped into his mind. Not long now and they would see the sun. But wasn't that rather premature? he wondered, glancing up at the swirling black fog that would engulf them even before they reached the top of the ice-wall.

And yet, amazingly, they never reached the cloud. As The Lion advanced up the ice-face, so the mist seemed to retreat. And when at last they hauled themselves up on to the snow-laden plateau at the top of the wall the cloud was still above them.

'How much further to the top?' Michael asked, sinking to his knees in the snow. He was thankful to have conquered the ice-wall.

The Lion turned to him, releasing from his belt the rope that had joined them from the beginning. 'We're not going to the top, Michael. Not yet, anyway.'

'What do you mean? The next bit looks easy.'

'For you perhaps.' He shrugged off his rucksack and dropped his ice-axe into the snow. 'Wait here.'

'But I – '

It was no use. The Lion had turned away and was walking across the plateau, looking all around him, as though searching for something.

It was then that Michael noticed the strange rock formation. Almost like a broken-down old . . . *bridge!* Was there an abyss just there? He stood up to look, his mind racing, his heart pounding. The legend! Where did fantasy end and fact begin?

Transfixed, he watched as The Lion approached the edge of the abyss, stopped short, and turned to face the mountain. 'I've come for you, evil one,' he called through cupped hands. 'It is the appointed time.'

Away to the left Michael saw a movement. A black rock, seemingly part of the mountain, dissolved before his eyes . . . and re-formed as a man. A tall, powerful man in the black garb of a monk – a man with flashing, devilish eyes. Muttering curses, the figure strode towards The Lion, his black boots churning the snow as an ice-axe appeared in his hand and he began slashing at the icy air.

'I have waited a long time for this moment, O favoured one,' he roared. 'Often I would have dared risk the Royal Guard to take a knife to your throat, just to see the King weep. But it matters not. This way will suit me fine. Your blood upon the snow will be a fine reward!'

'Perhaps that will be your undoing,' countered The Lion. 'For there are mysteries that not even a high-ranking servant in my father's courts would know . . . such as the power – the conquering power – that lies in the shedding of royal blood.'

'Then let us see!' growled the servant – and lifting the axe high above his head he hurled himself forward.

Michael gasped as the blade flashed down . . . and gasped again as The Lion grabbed the servant's wrist, stopping the axe short of his head.

'Die, curse you!' screamed the evil one.

But The Lion's hold was firm. 'Strike the blow and your own power is broken,' he cried.

'Lies!' raged the enemy. 'Just give me my chance!'

'You shall have your chance,' snarled The Lion, and with one mighty push he sent the black-robed figure crashing backwards to the ground. The axe went spinning from his hand, lost in the snow.

'Here!' shouted Michael, tossing his ice-pick to The Lion. 'You can beat him!'

The pick fell short and The Lion glanced quickly at the young mountaineer.

'I shall beat him, Michael, do not fear. But I'll have no need of weapons like that!'

Back on his feet the enemy approached again, snatching up Michael's pick and raising it to attack.

The Lion braced himself – and flung his arms wide.

'No!' screamed Michael.

The silver spike flashed – and plunged into The Lion's heart.

A shriek of pain echoed through the mountain peaks . . . but no cry had left The Lion's lips. Incredibly, though the enemy had struck the blow, it was he who had fallen and now lay writhing in the snow.

Staggering forward, blood pumping from his wound, The Lion reached down and grabbed hold of the enemy, clutching his waist-band with one hand and his hood with the other.

'Let me help!' shouted Michael, starting forward.

'Stay back!' cried The Lion. 'It is not yet finished.'

123

And with a sudden heave he swung the quivering body of the evil one high above his head. Turning to where an outcrop of rock was all that remained of the bridge, he moved steadily forward, then stopped, hurling the black figure from the plateau.

A deathly scream reverberated through the mountain as the body fell down and down into the abyss.

As Michael ran forward The Lion stumbled, his feet slipping on the icy outcrop of rock. At any moment it appeared he might follow the evil one into the narrow chasm.

'I'm coming!' yelled the young mountaineer, but already The Lion was toppling forward, crashing down across the broken bridge. Miraculously, his hands clawed hold of the tongue of rock jutting from the opposite side of the abyss . . . and he was safe, his body spanning the break in the bridge, his feet set into a hollow on one side and his arms entwined around the rock on the other.

Michael skidded to a halt in the blood-spattered snow. 'It's all right,' he cried, running out rope from a coil. 'You'll be safe once I've secured you to the rock.'

'No need,' breathed The Lion. He coughed weakly. '*Everything* is safe now.'

'But I – '

'Listen. You must do as I say, Michael. Return to the village. Tell what you have seen. Tell my father's people that I have opened up the way for them.' He paused, gasping for breath. 'And – and tell them to come.'

'But I can't leave you like this,' Michael protested.

'You must. This is the way it was meant to be, believe me. This was the *only* way. And now . . . now it is finished.'

Michael spoke again but his voice was lost in a crash of thunder. He glanced up at the swirling cloud still shrouding the highest peaks and suddenly was aware of a raging wind battering the mountain, ripping icicles from the jutting spurs and sending them splintering down the rock-face. A vicious storm was brewing. If he was going back to the valley he would need to start right away.

He glanced again at The Lion stretched out across the abyss, his face now grey and still, then turned and headed back to the ice-wall.

The storm lasted three days. Everyone said it was the worst the valley had ever seen and that it was a miracle that Michael was still alive. Some people, of course, questioned whether he and the stranger had ever climbed the mountain at all, and only old Franz believed his story that after descending the ice-wall he had been carried to the foot of the mountain on the crest of an avalanche. But it made for lively discussion while they were all waiting for the blizzard to blow itself out.

On the third day, however, all such talk was forgotten. For on the third day the sun rose! The cloud was gone. Wonderful, sparkling sunshine filled the valley. And everyone danced in the streets.

'And look! Up there!' cried Franz, shielding his eyes from the unfamiliar glare. 'Are those mountain peaks, or steeples of the old palace?'

Full of joy, the people pulled on their climbing-boots, drew on their coats, and headed up the mountain.

But this was not a hazardous climb. The avalanche had uncovered another route to the top: the old route, the gentle route that everyone from the youngest to the oldest in the village could manage.

'Just like it used to be,' muttered old Franz.

'And look!' exclaimed Michael when they reached the plateau. 'There's the bridge! There's where The Lion died . . . '

Or was it? Drawing nearer he was caused to wonder.

Ice had formed around the bridge, from one side to the other, and he wasn't at all sure that what he could see within the frozen formation was the body of a man or just solid rock.

But a child found the answer for him. 'Look, mister, the ice-wall is dark red underneath – can you see? Why is it red?'

Michael curled an arm round the boy's shoulders and found himself fighting back a sudden watering of his eyes. 'Because The Lion made this bridge for us,' he said. 'And it was a very brave thing to do because it cost him his life.'

The boy looked up at him. 'You mean that man is inside there right now?'

He hesitated. 'I'm really not sure. All I know is that he wasn't just any man. He was the King's son.'

'Mi-chael!' called a voice. 'Mi-chael! Up here!'

Together they all looked up. Far, far above them, high among the glistening peaks, a man was waving.

'But it can't be!' muttered the young mountaineer.

'Come on!' called the man, his voice echoing through the mountain. 'Follow me!'

They had hardly moved another step when something else caught their attention.

'Listen!' said Franz. 'Do you hear that noise? From up there somewhere!'

'Music?' gasped a woman. 'Up here in the mountain?'

'Maybe the King's having a party,' Michael laughed.

Then they turned and headed across the bridge, one by one climbing up into the sunshine . . .